THE BOY WHO
DREW THE FUTURE

RHIAN IVORY

Firefly

First published in 2015
by Firefly Press
25 Gabalfa Road, Llandaff North, Cardiff, CF14 2JJ
www.fireflypress.co.uk

ISBN 9781910080269
ebook ISBN 9781910080276

Cover artwork by Guy Manning
Cover design by Isabella Ashford

Typeset by Elaine Sharples

Printed and bound by: Bell & Bain Ltd, Glasgow

'Ask no questions, and you'll be told no lies.'
Charles Dickens, *Great Expectations*.

PROLOGUE

A twitching thing, it moves as if it were still alive.

But it can't be. The hand isn't attached to anything.

Sinews, veins and skin are dried up, discoloured, dead on the page. Yet it moves as if no one has told it. As if no one dares to say the word:

Drowned.

The boy draws it with his pen, line after line, unravelling the story that pulls him under, down into the dark water.

A hand forces itself up to the surface in his drawing, beckoning him or warning him, he can't quite tell yet. And no matter how hard he tries not to, he keeps drawing it.

The boy traces the watery lines of the past, the present and the future. With his pen shaking in his hand, he sleeps and draws, trapped between dreams and nightmares.

Twitching and twisting, he draws, as the tide waits patiently, ready to turn.

CHAPTER 1
NOAH

The barber doesn't try to engage me in awkward conversation as he cuts off my hair. I'm relieved he's a whistler not a talker as I try to make a different face look back at me in the mirror. He brushes the hair off the back of my neck and I attempt a scowl, narrowing my brown eyes, but it looks wonky. As I get up, I look down at the floor covered in light brown and blond hair. A haircut feels a good place to start.

Being the new boy again means I get to reinvent myself, I decide, as Mum buys me a new uniform at Fords department store. I try on more black trousers as she picks up a three-pack of white shirts, laughing with the saleswoman about my growth spurt. They talk as if I am not there. Mum keeps touching the back of my now naked neck as if she hasn't seen it in years. She tries to make the short hairs on my crown lay down flat, but then gives up and hands me a red and grey striped tie and two grey V-neck jumpers. They are itchy, not that I'll be wearing them in this heat. I wonder why she's buying them – *it is so hot.*

We moved to Sible Hedingham three days ago. Unpacking all our stuff into the plain, empty, rented house only took a day or two, and now I've ticked the last two items off my list I'm out of things to do. I leave Mum paying for my clothes and go outside. I walk around looking for something to fill the weekend quiet with. *Anything.* I mentally list all the things this new place has as I pass them: a butcher's, baker's, a DIY shop, a grocer's and a library next to a large primary school. It's a new place but still has the same 'please drive carefully through our village' signs. Large pots of pastel summer flowers are scattered around boasting 'Britain in Bloom' as I head up towards St Peter's Church. On a corkboard outside the Church are signs for the summer fete and a music festival, merging with peeling parish council notices about evensong.

Another wildnerness of normality, but this village has a feel about it. A prickling tingles in my fingers as I enter Broaks Woods. Something wants to be uncovered – I can smell it coming up off the river. There is something lurking here, whistling under the cover of the shady ash trees, hidden for now.

I sigh and shake it off. I don't want there to be any room or time for these feelings. I start walking faster, building up my pace, stretching my long legs out as I break into a run, heading down towards the river.

When we drive into the grey school car park on Monday morning, I wish I'd insisted on turning up on my own. I watch all the other students dragging themselves into school and realise that it's going to take more than a new haircut. They all look like they fit, like they know where they are going even if they don't really want to be here. I, on the other hand, have no idea, despite the déjà vu of Mum's monologue:

'I've explained about Dad's work and said that's why we've moved again. There's no need to go into details about why you left your last school, OK? This is another chance for you, Noah, a fresh start for all of us. Just *try* this time, sweetheart, please?' She switches the engine off, unclips her seatbelt and reaches across to squeeze my arm. Her bangles clang and clank in the silence. I have nothing to say so she carries on in a bright singsong voice, filling the hot car up with her hope.

'Now there's only the summer term left, so not long to go. You've got your exams next year ... so no more moving, right? We're staying put this time, aren't we?' She tries to make it sound like a statement or an order, but it comes out more like a question, her voice raising at the end as she looks at me. I nod and she sighs.

She tries to smile as she applies more lipstick, checking her reflection again in the mirror. I wish it were a real smile. I want to do more than just nod. She needs me to make her a promise, but I can't tell her a lie. I've tried before but I've never been very good at it.

I hold the door to the school open for her as the

receptionist buzzes us in. I wink at Mum as we wait in the entrance hall for someone to come and meet us. She tucks her short hair behind her ears and fiddles with her long dangly earrings and I whisper *'relax'* at her. She rolls her eyes at me. I want her to think it will be OK, that *I'll* be OK. The doors swing open and it begins. Again.

'Noah, here is your timetable, planner, some letters for Mum and a booklet on our codes of conduct.' They pile my arms high with things I don't care about or need, handing me lists of pointless rules I won't be able to follow. I imagine opening my arms wide and throwing all their stupid paperwork into the air, watching it fall like snow.

'Thank you,' I say, smiling widely at Mum as I give her a small wave goodbye. She walks away steadily, car keys in hand, and then I'm on my own. More people in sharp suits wearing photo ID tags around their necks introduce themselves. I smile again as their names and titles pour from my mind, spilling onto the hallway floor. I am guided to a classroom with a strong hand on my shoulder. A door opens and I am interred.

'This is Noah Saunders, he's joining us today. Make him feel welcome.' The heavy hand pushes me firmly into the room.

'Welcome, Noah. Right, back to work the rest of you. Find a free seat please.' The teacher returns to reading aloud from a book.

I can't hide from the staring faces in the silent room

I've interrupted. I hear a low wolf whistle and giggling from somewhere at the back and I know my skin will have flushed up blood red.

'Eva Hendries, please keep your catcalling and wolf whistling to yourself and *try ... try ... try* to act like a lady for once. Can you imagine Estella ever acting in this way? Miss Haversham would turn in her grave! Now, where were we...?' the teacher snaps at a girl with the long blonde hair and all the make-up and then picks up the story again. The class tunes back into the teacher's loud voice. I keep my head up, pretending to look like I know what I'm doing, and walk casually to the back of the room, having spotted one empty seat. I slide into it gratefully, but my knees crash into the table and I wince. I fold my legs under more carefully, trying hard to fit. Next to me sits a girl who is hiding under a lot of long messy dark hair. I peer at her through the curtain.

'Hi. I'm Beth,' she whispers, keeping one eye on the teacher. She reaches under her hair and flips it off her face so I can see her. She is small and dark-skinned with light brown eyes and her hair smells of lemons. She has tiny ears poking out of all her long black hair. The one nearest me is filled with silver earrings, nearly all the way up and round. Her lips are shiny, as if she's just coated them in lipgloss, and I can smell minty toothpaste on her breath. There are tiny white traces of it around her mouth. My hand moves upwards, as if to touch her lips with my fingertips. Instead I pull back, adjusting the pencil balanced on the top of my ear, as if I'm worried it might fall off. Adrenalin ricochets around my body. I nearly touched her! I'm supposed to be fitting in, blending into the background like a wallflower, not almost touching strangers who smell of lemons. I move my hands under the table and tuck them under my legs.

'I'm Noah.' I want to say something more interesting but am at a loss for words.

'Yeah, I know, Mrs Ashwell just said but, *Hi, Noah.*' She laughs softly at me and I can't help laughing back, a little. She's got one of those laughs that are contagious, like when someone yawns. I don't really know what we're laughing at but it feels good, better, more normal. Safer.

I watch her return to her work and get a pen out of my rucksack. I look up at the whiteboard, hoping for something straightforward and simple. A worksheet falls onto my desk and a battered copy of *Great Expectations.* I mumble my thanks. The teacher points at her wristwatch before stalking off again, her black heels clipping across the wooden floor like a metronome. I've forgotten her name already. I pick up the novel in relief. I've read it before; this should be easy.

'You'd better get on with it, or she'll keep you in over break, new boy or not.' Beth warns me, speaking behind her hand which has pen all over it. I can remember *her* name. The teacher is now staring at me from the front of the classroom, arms folded across her buoyant chest. I set my mind to finishing the worksheet before the bell. I don't want to be stuck in here with her over break.

When I get home from school, Mum is there, ready and waiting. I can smell baking. Clearly she hasn't got much work done.

'Come on, the suspense is too much. How was your first day? I thought you might text me at lunchtime? I haven't been able to do any work all day, not that I was worried, just … you know … wondering how you were getting on.' Mum flaps a hand in front of her face, as if to play down her concerns. She hands me a chunky slice of banana loaf and waits. I throw my rucksack to the floor and sit at the table. At least my legs fit under this one.

'It was alright. The English teacher is more than a bit *out there* but I liked History. I didn't get a chance to text you at lunch, sorry, it was all a bit full on.' I can't remember much more. I'm not withholding information, it's just there's not a lot more to tell, or at least not a lot more that I'm willing to tell, yet. I fill my mouth with the cake so I don't have to talk for a minute.

'Did you make any friends?' she says with such lightness that I can tell it's really important to her. I nod, swallowing the cake down. 'Yes. At least I think so. The girl who I sat next to in the first lesson, in English is OK. She's called Beth.'

I take a swig of the water. It's so cold it makes my teeth tingle. I need to get out of here. I don't want to talk about school any more, I don't want to play twenty questions or over-analyse every little thing I said or did. I get to my feet.

She and I speak at the same time.

'—Don't go up…'

'—I'm going up to get ready for my run…'

We laugh, not quite having steered around the awkward unsaid.

'Your dad's not here though. He's working on the Island. So make sure you take your mobile with you. *I know, I know,* but it makes me feel better.' She sips her tea. 'It's just I don't know your route or anything yet. In fact, why don't you skip your run and we could get a takeaway? I think I saw a Chinese on the high street. We could even watch one of your films, as long as its not that weird Beetle one again!' She grimaces, sticking her tongue out.

'*Beetlejuice* is a classic, Mum! OK, OK, we'll pick something when I get back? Maybe something vintage like *Edward Scissorhands*?' I offer, knowing she likes it almost as much as I do. 'What time's Dad getting back?' I move towards safer ground.

Her shoulders sag as she replies.

'Oh, late. It's going to be like this for a week or two, just while the project starts up. It'll calm down after that, hopefully.' She gathers up the plates, scattered with cake crumbs, and loads them into the dishwasher. As she rises I stoop down and kiss her on her cheek.

'Oh, if we're having a takeaway can you get me chicken balls, vegetable noodles, some egg fried rice and … um … definitely a bag of prawn crackers.' My stomach grumbles.

'Is that all?' she teases as I fill my water bottle from the tap.

'*Ha Ha!* See you in a bit.'

She carries on chatting, but I'm not really listening anymore. My hands have started shaking as I try to close the lid of the water bottle. When her voice begins fading away, I leave the kitchen quickly, stamping out the pins and needles in my feet.

It's starting, I can feel it.

I have to move. I need to get going.

I charge up the stairs to get changed into my kit and all I can think about is running away, running down to that river.

CHAPTER 2
BLAZE 1865

Dog always sensed someone arriving long before I did, giving me time to put away anything I didn't want prying eyes to see. There were enough of them in this village.

His black head lifted off his hairy paws and tipped slightly to one side as he sniffed the air. He lay back down across the doorway, in his usual position. Dog would bark long before anyone passed through the little gate or climbed over the fence if it got stuck in the heat. Most of them came that way to see me; hardly anyone came through the wild gardens, past the old Manor House. The house had been empty since the old man died leaving it to his three nephews, the men who turned Maman and me out.

They pushed us onto the street. Maman said they'd called her a *sorcière*, a witch, told her they'd heard the rumours in the village. The fat one pointed at the road to Halstead. 'Look for a tall building with gates and ask to see the Guardians, maybe they'll believe you when you write 'widow'! Or maybe they'll put you in a yellow jacket along with all the other sinners,' he shouted at us, laughing. They said more things about my father that I didn't understand, harsh-sounding words Maman wouldn't let me ask about. She waved my questions away, muttering curses under her breath as we stood outside wondering where to go.

Dog was snoring so I didn't think I had anything to worry about; all the same I packed my materials away into the box Emilia had given me.

Two summers ago, Emilia had found me down by the river the night Maman died. I'd run back, the whole long road from Halstead, stopping only when I got to the river behind the Manor House. She saw me as she came out from The Swan and she helped me up from the riverbank. She forced open the gate into the Manor gardens with a few kicks from her boots and then led me to this place, to my home.

'No one will think to find you in here. It's empty now up in the Manor. Must be a bit like coming home for you?' She helped me into the hut. She came back the next day with food and some clothes and asked me too many quick questions about Maman. She panicked when I told her it was just me and that Maman had passed.

'But who's going to help me now? That's why I helped you; I thought your mother would follow. Oh God, what will I do now? Will you help me? You could do it, couldn't you, lovey? You were always there when I came to see her, helping her, watching her. I'm sure you know as much as she ever did.' She talked on, convincing me to make her medicine, to take over from my mother.

I could see Emilia had deteriorated in the time we'd been gone. The rash was back on her left cheek like a red target mark and the swollen joints of her fingers looked sore. I knew there were plenty of dandelion roots and hawthorn hedges in the gardens that would help her and milk thistle and red clover were common enough anywhere. The disease was snaking its way across the left side of her face, which twitched as she spoke.

'You need looking after and, as you can see, so do I. I can't be seen like this. Your mother's cure was the only thing that helped. I need you, lovey. I need your help now.' She paused to look at me, waiting for me to say something.

'We can be friends, can't we, friends who help one another? I can keep your secret up here and you can keep mine under this hat. Please?' She pleaded with me as her thick red hands passed me a worn brown hat, a loaf of bread and a woollen blanket from her basket.

I wanted to help her; I could see she was in pain. So I said, 'Yes, I'll help you.'

I put the hat on my head. It fitted perfectly. I broke off chunks of the bread and ate and ate and ate.

Dog grumbled half-heartedly at the knock at the door. I got up slowly, allowing the uninvited guest time to turn tail and run if they wanted to, as they often did. I opened the door and was met with another hopeful face, another smiling girl from the village who wanted to ask me the same question they all did.

'I'm Mary Wright,' she told me, stepping over Dog. I'd seen her helping her father in the bakehouse. She handed me a brown paper parcel which was soft and warm in my hands. The hut filled with the smell of apples, cinnamon and peace. My stomach rumbled loudly as I sat back down and took my materials from the box. I was ready to help her see what she wanted to see: *her future*.

'Ask.'

She shifted from one foot to the other, unsteady now the moment had come.

'I wanted to know, I mean to say, I wondered if you could tell me something. Jacob Hill has asked me to meet him, has asked me to think on something he's said, or at least he's wanting to say and … I want to know if I should? Can you tell me if it's the right thing, to say … yes?' She found it hard to get her words out; she kept looking around me, past me, at the floor, checking the window and the shut door.

'Marriage?' I checked.

She nodded. Her cheeks flushed and she raised a hand to touch them.

My sharpened pencil flew over the page up and down, round and round. Circles and light and happiness bloomed on the page, shaping the lines that led to *yes*. It wasn't much; it was just a few shapes on a small square. I didn't have much paper left and wasn't sure when Emilia would bring me more, she hadn't been to see me for a few days now. Emilia always brought more paper when she came, hoping I'd show her something she wanted to see in her own future.

I passed the girl from the bakehouse the piece of paper and she ran her eyes over it again and again, nodding. I hoped she'd bring me another parcel from her bakery, but I knew to make this one last. She gave me a parting smile and skipped out of my door, tripping slightly over Dog, who refused to move. Dog padded over to me once she was gone and pushed his wet nose into my hand. I opened the parcel, tore the heel off the apple loaf and offered it to him, his soft mouth open wide as he swallowed it down, drooling. He waited for more, not knowing when he might be so lucky again.

You and me both, Dog, I thought, *you and me both,* as I threw another piece up into the air, watching him catch it like prey.

CHAPTER 3
NOAH

I spot her leaving the fruit section of the supermarket. I'm not sure whether to wave or pretend I haven't seen her. I'll probably be bumping into her all the way round. Now I've noticed her, it won't be easy to hide. I tap Mum on the arm.

'I'm just going to look at the DVDs. I'll catch you up.'

She nods absentmindedly and goes back to the honeydews.

I walk quickly now I've made my decision. I can hide from Beth at the back of the store until Mum has finished and then sneak out to the car park.

As I reach the top of the aisle, Beth is coming down it. She's laughing, trying to turn the corner, fighting a trolley with difficult wheels. A man tries to take the trolley from her to help, but she refuses to let him. Could be her dad, although they look nothing like each other.

'Hi. Beth? Hi,' I shout before I can stop myself and my arm lifts all by itself over my head in some sort of awkward wave. She sees me and, thank God, waves back. Then we both stand there.

She says something to her dad and he walks down the

aisle past me. He gives me a nod and then reaches behind me for something on the shelves. I move out of the way and walk towards Beth and even though this hadn't been the plan – this had been the complete opposite of the plan – I find myself smiling.

'I'm bored. Want to come and look at the films?' she asks and I nod.

'I warn you now, there's nowhere in the village to buy DVDs. They used to have a rental place but it shut down last year. *Gutted.* They used to do CDs too, me and Georgia and Eva were always in there. They had this ace little booth with headphones where you could listen to a couple of tracks before buying. I just download tracks now though.' She waits for me to say something.

'Everyone downloads stuff, don't they? I mean *I* don't, I still like CDs. I like the booklet thing you get at the front you know with pictures of the band and then the notes they write, thanking people and how they got their inspiration and stuff.' I follow her as if on some kind of autopilot, despite my brain shouting, *'Please make a U-turn when possible,'* over and over like Mum's stroppy satnav lady. Beth walks to the back of the supermarket where all the films are, trying not to get in the way of people charging around before it shuts. And my stupid feet just keep following her.

'Dad loves it in here. He likes to wait around until closing time, for the bargains. Mum's still at work, evening surgery,' she carries on as we scan the DVDs. I already know her parents are GPs because we've been doing family trees in History, another class we have together. Her mum's family are originally from Vietnam and her dad's family from Sible Hedingham. Her tree looked a total mess, especially when we had to add in what trades or professions our parents, grandparents and great-grandparents had, if we knew. Turns out my family are pretty ordinary, which is ironic. I have a milliner on my mum's side from Luton who made hats for royalty. My dad's side are slightly less interesting, all spending their time in foundries and down mines in Wales.

'My mum's the same. I lost the will to live in the fruit section. My dad's at work too. He's been at work since we moved here practically, which is doing my head in. It's not so easy running on your own, he kind of paces me. Mum's dropping me off at the woods on the way back.' I gesture to my shorts and running shoes to excuse my look. If I'd known she'd be here I'd have changed, I'd have at least put some wax in my hair or something.

'Nice that you do stuff together, you know, like a hobby. I'm sure it'll ease up once your dad settles in to his new job?' She's not bothered by my running gear.

'Maybe, he just gets easily distracted when he starts a new project. He wants it all to be perfect, wants everything to be just right, all the time. Like we're some happy little family!' I force myself to stop talking by rubbing my hand

19

over my mouth. I want to clamp it there to shut myself up but don't want to freak her out.

I have no idea why I am launching into my family's dynamic, standing in a supermarket on a Friday night with a girl I've just met. I don't talk about myself at all usually, at least not the real version. I normally stick a fake smile on my face and churn out the clichés that have always let me slot in unnoticed in the past. But this is new, this talking, and it has to stop. *I* have to stop.

'Sorry ... what?' I realise she's asked me a question. She is holding up a film. It looks awful. The cover is full of explosions, bits of debris flying everywhere and sweat-stained people in vests ducking for cover.

'I said is this your type of thing? What kind of films do you like?'

I shake my head, scanning the shelves for something half-decent. 'Not really. I've seen it though. I saw it with my dad at the cinema in ... umm, ages ago, when it first came out. It was predictable.' I shrug, hoping she won't ask me any more questions.

She has changed out of her school uniform and is wearing a fitted navy blue vest, short cut-off blue jeans and blue flip-flops. Her nails are painted a dark blue colour to match her vest, but it makes her hands and feet look almost dead. The air conditioning is a bit aggressive; Beth shivers as she puts the DVD back on the shelf. She spins back round to look at me, her long hair swinging into my arm, tickling it. She gathers it up in one hand, pulls a hairband off her wrist with her teeth and somehow manages to put it all up in a bun-type thing on the top of her head. Half of it falls out again and she tucks bits of it behind her ears, which are full of studs and sparkling hoops.

'It's freezing in here, isn't it.' She rubs her arms. I can feel my fingers twitching, wanting to touch her cold skin, to warm it, to wrap my hand around her wrist and hold her there. Instead I grab another DVD off the shelf, taking a small step away from her. I should leave. I should go. Just turn around and run. But she starts talking again and my feet become disconnected from my brain.

'Anyway, I'm not a big fan of action movies, but then I'm eclectic, apparently,' she carries on, oblivious.

'Oh? Who told you that?' I ask, an edge to my voice that sneaks in and surprises me.

'My parents. We have film nights on a Friday, well, not every Friday, depends what their surgery hours are like. Anyway, every other Friday I get to pick. Mum is a big musical fan which can be really hard going. Dad's more of a sci-fi geek which I can cope with.' She keeps taking films off the shelf, reading the blurb on the back and returning them to their place.

'Have you seen this one? Mum bought it for me to help with English. It's OK only because of Miss Havisham, it's the Helena Bonham Carter one, she's ace.' She moves closer to me holding out a shiny copy of *Great Expectations*. She still smells of lemons.

'Look, there's a bargain basement bin.' I walk over to it, putting some distance between us. There are always good finds in the bargain bin, films that have fallen out of favour or weird ones that never made it. They're normally pretty cheap too.

'Ah, I see you are eclectic too, Mr Saunders,' she says, gently pushing into me so she can look in the bin too.

'So how was your first week in Sible Hedingham?' she asks, rifling through the films. 'Nosy neighbours driving you mad yet?' she adds in a jokey voice, but keeps her sharp eyes on me.

'Not bad. I've had worse. Haven't met any neighbours though.'

I lift out *Gone with the Wind*. She shakes her head violently. So eclectic doesn't reach to the classics then.

'Oh, I thought she'd have been round by now, staking her claim, marking her territory and all that.' She begins fiddling with all the silver rings on her fingers.

'Who's *she*?' I don't like the idea of someone from school being too close. Last time Dad found us a house next to a field with no neighbours at all. Not that it made any difference in the end.

'Ah never mind, you'll see. So "had worse" … what do you mean? How many schools have you been to?'

And then I find it, what I'd been hoping to discover. A Tim Burton film.

'*Yes!* Now we're talking, this is more like it.' I hold it up for her approval, neatly sidestepping the question about schools, and all the other questions that will follow if I'm not more careful, if I don't watch my step and keep my mouth shut.

'Got it,' she declares, the smugness unmistakable.

'What? Are you kidding? No one I know's even heard of this.' I shake my head and look down at the copy of *Big Fish* in my hands. This is a first and it makes me stop, stop and really look at her.

'Eclectic! I did tell you. You can't go wrong with a Tim Burton film, can you. *Edward Scissorhands* is my all-time top favourite. It's my dad's turn to choose the film tonight so we're talking some zombie apocalyspe with spaceships but next time it's my turn ... you can come over, if you like? We'll watch *Big Fish*. So save your money,' she offers, talking and talking and talking while I stand there without a plan B.

'OK,' I answer quickly before I can change my mind, knowing I should take it back, drop the DVD, run back down the aisles and out of the door.

But I don't.

Instead I say OK again. I make it something definite, something new.

And something dangerous with her in the middle of it all.

'Ooops, sorry, love. Can't seem to get this thing to steer properly. Hi, I'm Sadie, Noah's mum.' My mum nearly runs into my foot with her trolley as she introduces herself to Beth.

'Hi, I'm Beth, it's nice to meet you. We were just having a look at the bargains.' Beth points at the film in my hand.

'Ah now, not more films, Noah? He took up nearly half the removal van with his boxes of films! Anyway we need to get to the checkout before they close. See you down there, Noah.' I watch her push the trolley off down the aisle and then turn back to Beth.

'So, see you later then?' My arm lifts again, as if it has a mind of its own. Why on earth do I keep waving at her? Why don't I just walk away and stop bloody talking?

'Sure. See you at school on Monday. Have a good weekend,' Beth says, perfectly in control of her own body.

She gently takes *Big Fish* out of my hands and drops it back into the bargain bin, leaving the touch of her skin on my hand like a mark.

CHAPTER 4
BLAZE

I waited until it was almost dark before pulling my hat down over my face to walk along the river path. It was the best time to go, to think and be by ourselves, just me and Dog. I took my time, whistling softly to myself, as I stooped low to pick up anything that caught my eye, a stone, a shiny bit of quartz sparkling in the fading light, something to add to my collection. I placed them around my hut to protect us from harm, a circle of special stones to keep us safe from the evil eye while we slept.

Maman wore a set of stones around her neck given to her by her mother and back through the generations. As a child, I used to wrap myself around her neck and hold them in my palms and wait for the heat to take over my body. These weren't plain stones like the ones in this river. *Pierres sacrées,* she called them, sacred stones from the river of her blood, from her family in France.

Maman's hot stones each had a tiny hole in the middle, not made by a human hand. She wore several of them on a leather string around her neck towards her end and when they didn't work, when even the stones couldn't warm her, heal her or hold her safe, I knew nothing would.

But I didn't show her what I'd drawn, what I'd already seen for her. I wanted to protect her from that pain.

She told me my father wore one of her sacred stones around his neck, that she had given him. But I didn't know this because I'd never met him.

He left before I arrived, so Maman said, sent back to sea as a punishment for falling in love with a French lady's maid, nothing but a servant. To teach him a lesson for stooping beneath him. But he didn't know about the seed that had been planted in Maman. He didn't know about the bloom in her belly, she promised me over and over.

As if that made any difference. We didn't need him, we were fine, just the two of us.

I buried some of her stones at the doorway to my hut. The others I kept around my neck, keeping her close to me. But what would happen to the sacred stones once I passed and started my next life? Maybe the river would claim them, taking them back where they belonged. Everything always came back to the sea, to the rivers that run on and on like Maman's stories.

Maman always had a tale to tell me while we worked, cleaning the Manor House with brushes and soap. I asked her questions about my father, but instead she turned to her own family and the legends of the Ambroise women, the wise water women of Couesnon.

'The Ambroise women have always been visited by those who need help. They always come to the women born in the river Couesnon. Our family are water babies born in the river and this makes us wise, *femmes sage*. I must have told you the tale of Mont Dol, the little island and our river, the river Couesnon?' she would ask and I would shake my head every time, wanting the story again, needing to hear the music in her voice.

'Well now, listen carefully, come closer, *mon chéri*. This is the story I heard from my Maman and she from her Maman before. They say *Le Diable*, the Devil, was furious when Mont Saint-Michel was built and full of hate towards *Saint Michel* for the monastery they gave him.' I knew what came next, almost by heart, but waited as she spun the story.

'*Le Diable* and *Saint Michel* agreed to compete for ownership of the Mont. Whoever could jump the closest to the island would win. But *Le Diable* fell into the River Couesnon, going down and down into the dark water. The last they saw of him was his hand clawing up through the water. And then nothing. *Disparu!* Gone! But *Saint Michel?* Well, the air lifted *Saint Michel* up into the sky like a nightingale, singing out all the way to Mont Dol, where he was set down on safe ground under the stars.'

I could feel my mouth was open as I listened. She smiled and carried on, nearing the end of the tale.

'Some say that at the top of Mont Dol there is a footprint of *Saint Michel* and at the bottom, on the rocks, the bloody red claw marks of the *Le Diable*. Beware *Le*

Diable sitting at the bottom of the river ready to pull you down by your ankles and gobble you all up!' she would warn, half serious and half not, and I never forgot. I knew the power that her stories held; they were always more than just tall tales to entertain me.

Dog started pacing up and down in the river barking up at me. *No fish or food in there, a pebble won't fill your belly.* He's caught a few fish in his time, Dog, one or two from the Long Pond which I had to prize from his mouth and throw back in. Maman always made sure those fish were safe and looked after. She called them her rainbows. They had a strange name, one I'd never heard before and couldn't quite say, but the old man had been fond of them and so I showed them the respect they were due.

Dog came to stand next to me, panting as quietly as he could in the heat. There was no one else around, but the bats would be out soon, the light was going fast. I looked across the river to the other side, wondering whether we'd have better luck over there, when I saw something. It was in the middle of the river close to the Island, half covered. I screwed my eyes up to make sure, but I knew what it was as soon as I saw it.

It was a hand. A hand reaching up out of the water, pointed upright but not moving. The fingers were pressed together with no gaps, all closed up, and the palm was steady. It didn't stir as the rapids flew around it. *Stop*, it said. *STOP. Don't come any nearer, don't move an inch, just stand there.* So I did – and then the light changed and it was gone.

It was as if it had fallen back into the water or had never been there in the first place. I looked at Dog to see if he'd seen it, if he'd waited with me. He was chasing another fish, diving down into the water, his tail going back and forth swishing the river at our feet so that I couldn't see the bottom any more.

I couldn't see anything but the stars, as the bats above started their nightly battle with another murder of crows.

CHAPTER 5
NOAH

The bell rings for break. Everyone jumps to their feet and then sits back down again as Mr Hambleton, the D&T teacher, launches into a sarcastic speech about the meanings of bells. Then to make matters worse he starts singing, playing air guitar.

We are all silent until Theo starts a slow clap. Everyone copies, especially Harley who takes it one step further, standing up, holding his hands above his head as if he's at a gig. Theo gives him an approving nod and stands up too. I clap but stay in my seat. Mr Hambleton doesn't seem to mind and even takes a bow. He pretends to hold a guitar up and does some rock god power stance as we hurriedly put away our materials.

'Metallica, music of the gods I tell you, lyrics of kings! YouTube it and learn a thing or two about *ROCK!*' he shouts at us as we run away.

'And no running in the workshop, how many times do I have to say the same thing? It's like talking to a brick wall. *Just another brick in the wall!*' He starts singing again as we escape into the corridor, leaving him to rock it out alone.

Beth meets me outside the D&T room next to our

lockers. Theo and Harley high five each other and charge up the corridor chanting, *'METALLICA! METALLICA! METALLICA!'*

'Ah, I see you've met the god of rock. You got off lucky, last term he bought his guitar in and made us listen to him play. You should have picked music; I've just had a double which was ace.' Beth holds up sheet music which looks mad and makes no sense. She's written all over it or drawn symbols and notes in pencil. Her hands are covered with notes and ink too.

'Are you writing something?' I ask impressed.

'Not writing! *Composing!* I can't wait till my piano lesson tomorrow.' She clutches the paper to her chest as if it holds a secret.

'So can I hear your masterpiece? What's it like?' I breathe out too loudly, instantly regretting my question.

'Sure. Well, maybe, when I'm finished. I need to practise a bit more first. You'll just have to wait and see.' She opens her locker, tucking the sheet music into a folder and shuts the door firmly. I can wait, there's no rush.

I open my locker and reach in to get my drink and crisps, but most of the contents fall out onto the floor as soon as I open the door. There's hardly any room in the corridor to reach down and pick up my books and food. Beth kneels to help me gather up my stuff before it gets trampled in the break-time stampede. She passes me my text books.

And then I see it on the floor. I try to pick it up before she notices, but I'm just not quick enough.

'What's that … drawing? I thought you had D&T not Art.' Her inky hand touches the paper, about to turn it over to see better.

I jump as if I've been burned and snap, '*Don't!*' at her in a low voice which doesn't belong to me. I throw my hands over hers and my paper, covering up everything I can. My hands throb as she whips hers out from under mine, looking stung.

There's noise all around us, shouting, laughing, some screaming and singing. I can hear music coming in and out as doors open and slam shut, a teacher shouts and someone nearly trips over the pair of us crouched on the floor in front of the lockers. I try to say sorry with my eyes, before looking down at my drawing.

I rock back on my heels with relief when I see what I've drawn. *It isn't anything bad.*

I offer her a smile and breathe out, then tip forwards grabbing everything off the floor, including the drawing, and shoving it all back into my locker as best as I can with my cramping fingers.

My hands hurt, but it doesn't matter now. It isn't anything bad. I haven't drawn anything bad.

It's just a hut, like a small wooden shed with a slanted roof sloping down into a mass of ivy. The hut is bordered by daisies and tall grass. It has two windows with no curtains in and the glass is cracked. The door is ajar, but I haven't drawn anything inside. It is empty, like someone has just left. *It's all fine.*

I don't know what to say to her. I can't let this awkward moment linger, as we stand in front of my locker not sure what to do next. I pretend to check I've locked it properly but my fingers won't work, I can't hold the key steady. She's staring at me. I can feel the heat of her gaze, but I can't look at her yet. I don't know what she's seen or if it means anything, but the stare is long enough to make me shove the key deep into my trouser pockets where I keep my hands, out of sight.

'Hey, Beth, are you coming then? We need to get to the benches before they all go. Or are you busy here with the new boy, *Noah*? Sam's meeting Georgia there, but if we don't hurry up he might take the chance to leg it. *Again!*' The tall pretty blonde girl with heavily made-up blue eyes stands in front of Beth towering over her. She looks at me, smiles sweetly and then sticks out her arm to Beth. The other girl, presumably Georgia, is rolling up her already short skirt. She stops and scowls at Eva.

'Eva, just shut up about Sam, OK!' Georgia sticks out her tongue. Her lipstick is so dark it almost looks black, which doesn't quite work with her freckles and bright red hair.

'Personally I think you should go for Harley. He's much more your type, Georgia, as in fit and actually interested in you. Sam's so quiet and not really into redheads, at least that's the excuse he gave last time he stood you up!' Eva puts as much disgust into her voice as she can on the words 'quiet' and 'Sam'.

I stand there, unsure what to say, while Beth makes her mind up. I want to say sorry, to keep her next to me, but now she won't look at me. I can't string a sentence together, there's nothing in my head, other than the beat of the blood slowly bringing the feeling back into my hands. I watch her take each girl's arm, then the three of them turn and walk off as one. United.

'See you later, *neighbour*!' Eva turns back and shouts at me and then there's more laughing and shoving and Sam, whoever he is, gets a few mentions, some good and some bad.

Eva looks over her shoulder at me as they reach the doors. They step out into the sunshine and she gives me another little smile, but this time it isn't a nice one.

CHAPTER 6
BLAZE

The door creaked open, sticking on the lintel. It had grown too big in the heat and didn't fit as it had in the winter. Emilia snapped me out of my worries as she forced the door open with her wide hip.

'I've brung you some more clothes, not that you've grown any, but a few more layers won't hurt, lovey.' Emilia took out a bundle of browns and blacks from her basket and set them down on the small table with a sigh of satisfaction.

'Thank you,' I said as I reached out to touch the material. It was coarse and thick but would be of use when the weather turned. She settled herself down on my stool leaving me to stand. Dog turned about a few times then crouched uneasily by the doorway, keeping his head up and his eyes open.

'How have you been then?' she asked, as if we were neighbours meeting at church on Sunday.

'Fine.'

She sighed. 'Not much of a talker, are you? It's a good job I haven't come for a chat. Can't that hound sit outside while I'm here? I don't want to get ill again. Who knows how many ticks he's got on him. Filthy animal.' She scowled at Dog, as if he and he alone were to blame for her ailment.

I clicked my tongue and Dog got to his feet slowly and skulked out of the hut, as if to make a point. I knew he was clean, I checked him myself, but I could understand Emilia's reaction. She smiled warmly at me once we were on our own and I smiled back as she got to her feet to shut the door and keep Dog out.

'Now I think I have something in here for you. Where is it?' She rifled through her wicker basket, muttering to herself, and then set a parcel on the table next to the clothes. The small hut filled with the smell of meat and pastry.

'Here it is. A nice pie, baked it myself just for you. Might put some meat on you, you're all skin and bones, lovey. Help yourself then,' she offered peeling off the muslin as the scent and spices filled my nostrils. My stomach grumbled loudly and she laughed out loud.

'Go on then, eat up.' She prodded me, laughing gently, and I couldn't stop myself. Dog had crept back in, following his nose, and was watching my every move. Mouth watering, I reached out to pick up the pie she'd kindly made me and share it with Dog when she slapped my hand, hard.

'*Ah ah*, not yet. Not just yet.' She wagged her finger playfully at me. 'Now then, why don't you get that little box out and we'll see what's what, shall we? Have a little look to see what's round the bend for me?'

Her voice was light and soft but I could hear what was lurking underneath. I could sense her eagerness as she sat forwards on the edge of the little stool eyeing up my box under the table. She couldn't keep away. Sometimes I wished she would. I'd happily go without her pies and clothes if it meant I could keep from her the bends in her road. I didn't want her to see what I had seen. No one should see such an end.

'Come on now, don't be shy, lovey. It's just us friends after all, just a bit of give and take, and now it's your turn. *So give me what I want!*' she snapped at the end, all the lightness and softness gone from her voice.

Dog grumbled low and tense, getting to his feet as I reluctantly pulled the box out from under the table.

She smiled, realising I'd given in and began to cut up the pie, but I'd lost my appetite.

I couldn't have eaten a thing.

CHAPTER 7
NOAH

'Come on in,' Beth invites me, pushing open her front door. We step into a long, narrow tiled hallway with steep-looking stairs at the end. She puts her keys down on a dark round table and walks off into another room. I follow. I wasn't sure if she'd want me to come back to her house after the weird non-argument we'd had by the lockers yesterday, but we'd been paired up in Mr Bourne's class for our History project on village life. This was fine with me, better than fine, in fact. It wasn't like anything had happened, not really, but I needed to take more care. I didn't want anyone getting hurt.

I shouldn't even be here, dragging her into my troubles, but I didn't speak up in History. I didn't ask for a different partner, or suggest we did our homework in the library at school. Because I didn't want to. I wanted to be normal, to say, 'Yeah, sure, let's go back to your house,' as if it were nothing, as if I did this kind of thing all the time. I didn't seem to be able to stop myself from saying yes to her.

'Do you want to go outside and make a start? I've got Mum's Polaroid and you can have my digital camera if you want. We could try and get a view of the river from the back gate? There's a path down to the river. Or we could take some of the fish in the pond?' she asks, putting the lid back on the now empty cake tin.

'Sure. Can I ask you something first? Does your friend Eva live near me?'

She passes me a bottle of coke from the fridge, which I take gratefully.

'Yep. She's staked her claim, said she saw you first. Told us all about you the day you moved in, before you started school. I got a long text that described you from head to toe and back again in full technicolour detail.' Beth steps out into a tangle of garden. I follow, taking care not to trip over the step. The garden is in lots of different parts. I can't see it all or where it ends. It is wide, quiet and very overgrown in places. We stop in front of a rectangular long pond tucked underneath some shady ash trees.

'Thought I'd seen her around the estate, near my house, *a lot* in fact,' I reply, feeling uncomfortable.

'Well, she lives right behind you, says she can see your bedroom window from hers. Eva says you go running every night. Don't look like that, she's not a stalker. She just said you looked *fit*, or words to that effect, but I don't want to make you blush. Maybe you should draw your curtains before you get changed next time though.' She smirks, clearly amused at how awkward this is making me. It wasn't the thought of someone seeing me getting undressed that bothered me. I was more worried about the fact that she was watching me at all. She'd picked me out as someone to take notice of. I hadn't ever thought about someone watching *me*, it was usually the other way round. *Shit.*

'Anyway, don't panic, don't look like that! Theo asked her back out again last week, so you're safe, well, for now anyway.' Beth laughs at my face. I must look terrified. I try to rearrange it. People like Eva make me nervous.

'Have you been friends for a long time then?' I take a picture of Beth as I ask, hiding my face behind the camera.

'No, well, sort of. I mean we used to be really good friends, the three of us, but it's been a bit weird this last year. Eva's really changed, since she started seeing Theo. She's with him and Harley all the time now and some others in the year above. They go down to the church at night and hang out in the graveyard.' Beth stops talking and shivers.

'Why?' I can't think of anywhere less inviting.

'Good question. Dunno, somewhere to go I guess. They do these dares…' She stops and sighs.

'Right, dares. Do you do them? I mean, go down to the graveyard at night?' I feel concerned for her, but more than that I feel left out, as if she's been having another life with Theo, Harley and Eva, in the dark, at night, doing dares.

'No way! I'm … I'm not scared of the dark or anything embarrassing like that but … *I'm scared of the dark!*' She bursts out laughing, then puts both her hands over her eyes.

I don't laugh at her. I know what lurks in the dark. She's right to be scared.

'Don't tell anyone, will you? I've never told anyone that before. I thought I'd grow out of it. No idea why I'm telling you now … *awkward.*' She peeks through her hands, her eyes narrowing as if she's deciding whether she can really trust me. I want her to know she can, so I nod several times to reassure her. I'd never laugh at someone else's fears.

'So what kind of fish are these anyway?' I ask, wanting to change the subject, to put her at ease. I hold the camera up and look at the fish. I'm expecting goldfish or carp not these small pockets of colour, whip thin and fast moving.

'Shubunkins. They've been here since the Manor House was first built, obviously not these actual fish but their ancestors. It's a tradition or something; there'll always be Shubunkins at the Manor House. Apparently it's really bad luck not to have them, according to my dad. He believes in all that kind of stuff, knocking on wood, saying "bless you" after you sneeze and keeping up with old village traditions. That's what comes of living in the same place all your life.' She pauses to wave a square photo around, waiting for the sun to dry the image. We watch it develop, the fish forming in front of our eyes like the strokes of paint on canvas.

'Georgia and I've got fed up with her, Eva, I mean. She's desperate to match me up with Harley! I know, *Harley!*

41

She keeps bugging me about going down to the graveyard so I can see what a laugh it is. I've said my parents won't let me, but I haven't even asked them. I don't like Theo, I just don't trust him, not when he's with Harley and Jay. Sam's alright though and Georgia, sometimes, but she just does what Eva says, whatever Eva dares her to.'

Beth gets up and starts towards a small green gate at the back of the garden. She keeps playing with her necklace as we walk along. A thin black band hangs around her neck with a stone threaded on it through a tiny hole. It looks pale and warm against the colour of her skin.

'You don't have to do anything you don't want to do. No one can make you,' I say, wishing it were true. I unlock the gate and hold it open for her and she nods half-heartedly as we make our way through the buttercup-filled field down to the river.

I know how easily things can get out of hand and how hard it is to turn from what's in front of you. Fate. Destiny. The Future. Whatever you want to call it. Unless you run fast, keep running and don't turn around to see who or what's behind you, it'll find you.

It'll find you, catch you and trip you up until you stumble and fall.

CHAPTER 8
BLAZE

A man came this morning. *A man.* He came before it was light, before anyone could see him. He must have walked blindly up the river path because he carried no lantern. He didn't even knock, just opened the door and walked in. He shook me awake in his panic and Dog barked.

'Help me,' he instructed.

I rubbed my eyes and looked past him to see if he was alone. He was a big man filling up the room. He had a dark coat on but no hat. He looked as if he'd left quickly, as if he'd run here. I began to speak, to ask him what he wanted, when he grabbed me. He pulled me to my feet and shook me, accidentally stamping on my bare toes with his heavy boots.

'Wake up. Get up, boy. I need you. My child is ill, *my girl*. Please, my wife said you'd help us. She said you'd know what to do.' His voice began firm and hard but changed, breaking into silence. He held out a lump, bound in plain cloth and tied with string. I thought it was the child and shook my head quickly, stepping away from him and it. He pushed the bundle into my arms and I opened it, relieved to find bread and cheese, a bottle of beer and a pair of boots. They were brown leather men's boots with thick laces. He looked down at my dirty feet and gestured to the big boots.

'My wife told me you'd help us. Put them on and come with me? Please?' He was crying, wiping his face on his sleeve.

I said, 'Yes, I'll come, I'll help you.' What else could I do?

He waited for me to gather herbs, vials and my small knife, which I shoved into my coat pocket. He watched in silence as I put on the boots. They didn't fit; they were men's boots, probably once his. But they were still boots and I had none. I pulled the laces as tight as they'd go. I reached for my hat, put it on and told him, 'Go.' He pushed open the door and ran to the fence. Dog and I followed him down the dark river path towards his child.

He stopped in front of the farrier's cottage and pushed open the door. As I walked into the cottage I recognised the woman who must be the farrier's wife. She never told me her name when she came to see me, but I remembered her now; she had a strange voice, as if she wasn't from these parts. Her skin had cleared up well leaving only a few scars on her forehead.

She stood next to a low cot which had a child in it. She didn't look at me but cried out, 'Oh bless y'pet, bless y'for coming. I didnae know what to do. *Ma wee girl, ma wee girl.* I canny wake her up.' She pulled me into the room,

44

taking my hands, leading me to her child. I took off my hat and knelt by the small cot. It held a little girl with long white hair. Her chest was moving up and down too fast, her breathing shallow and wet. A pile of blankets lay at her feet. There was a small fire in the hearth and the front door was still wide open.

'Shut the door, we need to keep her warm. And build the fire,' I instructed. She looked quickly at her husband and then back at me.

'Mary said y'd know what t'do. Mary Wright told me t'send Thomas t'you. She told me where y'lived.' She folded her arms across her chest as if to challenge me, as if to say, 'Go on then give me away,' but I didn't. I would never do that. Instead I reached past her and pulled the blankets up over the child.

'But she's burnin', she's on fire.' She put out her arm as if to stop me.

'Leave him be, Aileen. Just leave the boy be. He knows what to do, let him help us,' her husband shouted, and then turned to the fire to build it up.

'Hot water,' I called out and she rushed over to the fire to get some from the pot. I shut the door. There were coats hanging on pegs next to it. I gathered them up. I placed these behind the child's back to lift her up. The gurgling in her throat eased and her chest began moving up and down at a slower pace. I cleared a space at their table, knocking things onto the floor. I emptied my pockets, took out my knife and cut a piece of fennel then mixed in some chamomile. The woman placed a jug of hot water on the table next to me and returned to her child, stroking the damp hair off her face.

I took a bowl and added some water to the mixture to dilute it. It bonded quickly forming a thick paste. 'Put it on her chest,' I called to the woman, who took the bowl from me. I took a shirt from a pile of clothes on a chair and tore it into thin strips. 'Wrap them around her, tight.'

The man handed them to the woman. I dropped some nettle and ginger tincture from a vial into another bowl, diluting again with hot water.

'Spoon?' I asked. The man found me one. I took the bowl over to the child's bed and put it on the floor. I held her gently, pulling her up. She fought me weakly, trying to push me away. I fed the mixture into the child's mouth, telling her, 'It's good. Good for you.'

When it was empty the man took the bowl away and then came to stand at the foot of the cot. I held the girl tightly in my arms and we all watched and waited, none of us making eye contact at all. In my arms I held their precious gift and I felt the pressure, the possibility that this might not work. But I had to have faith. The man stood over us, his daughter and I, and I felt his trust in me and hoped and prayed that the girl wouldn't get worse.

Within minutes her eyes widened and she leaned over

and started retching violently, struggling for air as fluid flew out of her mouth, spattering us and the bed.

'What hae y'done? What hae y'done? Get off, *shift yerself!*' the woman screamed at me, pulling her daughter out of my arms.

The child started to cough up clotted green lumps, spit hanging greasily from her gaping mouth. She paused in between the heaves to cough and hack, bringing up more phlegm, the smell of which turned my stomach and filled the hot room. After this she collapsed back on the bed, but there was colour in her cheeks and her face had changed shape.

'Keep her up. Push her up,' I told the man and he gathered her small form in his arms and sat behind her so that she couldn't fall back.

'Give more of this, one spoon in water, three times a day.'

The man nodded and then whispered, *'Thank you,'* but couldn't tear his eyes from his wife and their child.

The child looked at me, the only one in the room who would, then closed her eyes and fell asleep, breathing soft and steady in her father's arms.

CHAPTER 9
NOAH

'What's that tune you're whistling? Sounds really familiar,' I ask Beth as we walk further up the garden, away from the Manor House. Beth had been whistling under her breath all day at school, moving her fingers up and down on the desk.

'I wasn't... I didn't know I was. *Sorry*. I've been practising that piece I wrote. There's a bit I can't get right. It's probably that section I've been whistling.' She rubs her hand across her nose as we walked under the ash trees.

I can play music in my head too. I can select a track and press an imaginary play. I'll hear it in my head, but I'd stop myself from whistling it out loud. I have to take steps to make sure I don't stand out, don't draw stares or start people whispering behind their hands. Making yourself blend into the mass of white shirts and ties, acting as normal and uniform as possible, results in an easier life.

We'd been going back to her house every day after school to take more photos and try and pull together a decent presentation for the first part of our History project. We'd decided to focus on animals in the village, rather than people or buildings. We'd managed to get a few pictures of the kingfishers on the river, which would look great if we blew them up big enough. We'd have to go to the church at dusk to stand any chance of catching the barn owl that had been seen in the graveyard. We hadn't picked the easiest subjects to take decent photos of – all the animals kept moving, blurring the pictures.

Dull weeds sulk around the edges of a small hut as we reach the top end of the garden backing onto bright yellow fields in flower. The shabby building leans awkwardly against a walled area that must have once been full of herbs.

'It smells of chamomile and mint.' I sniff the air and take photos of the honeybees collecting pollen from the flowers, hoping to get some useable ones.

'There *was* a herb garden, I think, in the olden days, when it was a proper Manor House. I should think there was a housekeeper, a gardener and a cook, maybe more. Clearly there's no gardener working here now or any other servants!' She laughs, pointing at a crumbling wall leading off to long rows of rectangular vegetable beds. She laughs a lot, finding things funny and light. She's so easy to be with. She doesn't look at me with a fleck of fear in her eye, she just smiles and tells me more about the history of her house.

'Dad says this place was empty for years and years before someone in his family inherited it. Blames the state of the garden on that rather than the fact that he and Mum haven't got a clue. They keep talking about getting a goat, but I think it's a joke, at least I hope it's a joke!' Beth tries to open the door but it's stuck, possibly swollen in the heat. It is unbelievably hot.

'Told you. This place is falling apart, nothing fits anymore. All the windows have gaps in them. You should hear the wind howling in the winter. Mum and Dad refuse to replace the sash windows with PVC ones. They say we are guardians of the house and have to keep it as it was.' Beth manages to free the door after a few awkward goes and holds it open for me. We sit down on some wicker chairs which are even more uncomfortable than they look.

'So where did you live before here?' Beth asks, putting the heavy Polaroid camera down on the table.

It is an ordinary question, one I'm used to answering, used to lying about, but the words get stuck in my throat. I cough and open my bottle of water, taking the first long cold gulp.

'All over the place. Dad's a wildlife photographer, so he works for different companies and magazines. Mum says she doesn't mind all the UK moves, but says she's not leaving this country. I like the idea of going off somewhere exotic. In fact, Dad's been offered work with the coastal path project on Anglesey, not that an island in the Irish Sea exactly fits my idea of exotic! Mum's not keen, she says the only weather they get in Wales is rain.' Rain sounds quite nice right now in comparison to this relentless heat.

Beth looks pityingly at me, as if this is the worst idea she's ever heard.

'You'd be so cut off though, wouldn't you, living out there on an island? I can't imagine living somewhere different, or moving about all the time. I don't mind travelling to see Mum's family or going on holiday, but I love my home. I'd never want to live anywhere else but here.' She wriggles in her chair as if the thought makes her uncomfortable.

'It's alright, you get used to it. Dad gets to do some interesting stuff, he says it's better than being stuck in an office. He's working with the RSPB on Wallasea Island documenting their wild coast project, you know, like a photographic record of everything they do. I don't mind really and I like new places and meeting new people,' I lie, dipping my head away. I take the pencil off my ear and begin doodling on some old seed packets on the table.

'Anyway, that's enough about me, we're supposed to be taking photos for History. I think we need a few more of the church and the owl you said you saw. Want to take some more of your famous fish?' I ask her, needing to change the subject. I don't want to talk any more about myself or where I've been or why we move so much.

'We should have asked your dad if he's the expert on photography,' Beth suggests.

'*No!* I mean, no way, we can't cheat. That'd put us at an

unfair advantage, nope, we've got to do this on our own. Just you and me.' I kick her foot gently with mine and she kicks me back, grinning.

'OK, OK, no cheating. But we could ask him for a bit of help? I've got absolutely no idea how to take a decent shot of an owl at night! Shall we go back to your house tomorrow instead of here?' she says, not willing to let it drop, sitting back on the wicker chair which cracks.

I don't want to put my mum and Beth in the same room. I don't want Mum watching us, looking at me, building up questions about this to bombard me with later. I'm not ready for that. I don't even know what *this* is yet.

I put the pencil back on the top of my ear and look at the brown paper seed packets on the table and shiver despite the heat. I've covered them with drawings of her fish, using up every millimetre of space with fins and eyes and tails. I hold them up to the sunlight from the open doorway to see better. The paper is thin, almost see-through, like fish scales. There's something funny about them, they look weird and at odd angles.

Beth follows my gaze.

'You like drawing, don't you? You're always doodling in class. So why didn't you pick Art? Why did you pick D&T?' She leans out of her chair a little trying to see what I've been sketching. I lower the papers, moving them away from the sun.

'Oh, I promised my parents I'd pick a proper subject, you

know, something you can use to get a proper job. Don't think the scruffy Art student would cut it for Mum and Dad.'

I remember the conversation I'd had with my parents as we left our last house, as we were handing the keys back to the letting agency. In the car outside the estate agents, I promised them once again that I'd stop drawing, that I'd hide my pictures better and I wouldn't bring them into the next school. I heard my voice telling them I would not try to warn anyone about anything because, as my mum said in a surprising moment of bluntness, no one ever believed me anyway.

Not until it was too late.

My parents had no idea how much I meant to keep the promise, how much I tried to stick to my word, but I just couldn't. And here was the evidence, right now, all over these seed packets. The drawing would take me over anywhere and everywhere these days, sometimes even without my hands shaking to warn me. My vow to my parents seemed pointless, like a child's promise, earnestly made and easily broken.

I jump up and shove the packets into my back pocket.

'C'mon, let's go back down to the pond and take some photos. We should get something done. Does it smell funny in here to you? It's giving me a headache.' I'm telling the truth, the temperature in the hut is oppressive, making the room smell strongly of something I don't recognise. It reminds me of garlic but it's not quite so familiar.

'Yeah, sure. Let's go then.'

She bangs into the table sending my bottle crashing to the floor. She sounds sharp. I pick up the bottle and then stand away from the door to let Beth go first. She pushes past me slightly, looking cross. As I follow her out, I trip over something in the doorway.

'Oh!' I shout, falling over my feet, startling a group of nightingales. A watch, they're called, a watch of nightingales, which makes sense – it feels like they are watching me as they spiral up into the air.

'What's up now?' she asks, turning back to look at me, hands on hips, and I feel stupid sprawled over the grass, staring up at the noisy birds.

'Nothing. Just tripped.' I jump up, feeling embarrassed, and look down to see what I've fallen over. I'd caught my foot on the worn, flaking threshold of the hut. I crouch down and try to push the splinters of wood back together, feeling guilty that I've damaged the doorway. As I push the wood into the earth, I feel a lump, a hard uneven edge at the base of the hut. I scrape away with my nails, which tingle as if I've been stung by nettles. My hand wraps around something small and rounded and hot. It is a stone covered in mud, but I can see it isn't just a lump of gravel or concrete or brick. I wipe it on my school trousers and hold it up in the sunlight. It gleams fiery in the heat of the sun.

'What's that?' Beth asks, reaching her hand out. I hold the soft stone in the palm of my hand for her to see. She looks at it and smiles.

'You've found another stone! Look, it's just like mine.' She pulls her necklace out from under her white shirt to show me and the stones match perfectly. Pale, soft, rounded and hot to touch. They are a matching pair.

I close my fingers back around the stone, hiding it. It feels like I've pressed my palm up against an oven door. It is so hot that it feels cold for a split second, as if I've got frostbite. Then a spicy warmth runs through my skin, down into my veins, and rockets around my whole body. I tingle again as many different smells, tastes and sounds fill my senses.

I close my eyes, my head whirling, forgetting Beth, her garden and the hut. I hear a tune whistled in a high pitch which cuts through the air like a signal. It sounds like the watching birds in the trees above trilling in their secret language. I open my eyes.

Beth is soundlessly watching me, holding her hand out for the stone which I don't want to give her. But it isn't mine to keep.

My fingertips bump against hers as I drop the stone into her hand. When I pull away I feel cold and alone in the silence, the whistling long gone, carried away on the breeze of the birds' wings.

CHAPTER 10
BLAZE

'They've been gone a while now. I don't normally fret but Alfie and I argued just before he left. To be honest I didn't want him to go, I asked him not to, at least not until after we were wed. I just need to know if he's coming back to me. He's taken my brother Daniel with him this time. Reckless the pair of them, don't care a jot for me or Mother and our worries.' She didn't wring her hands in her lap, or look past me, or keep an eye out for someone else coming. It was as if she was beyond all of that, as if she didn't care who saw her sitting on my stool, in my hut. She wore a white apron over her black dress which smelt faintly of woodsmoke. She pushed Dog gently with the heel of her boot, rubbing his side as he lay at her feet. None of the others ever seemed to even notice Dog, or me, too set on what they'd come for.

'I'll show you,' I promised her, hoping I'd be able to. I didn't know her name but I'd seen her before, heading out across the parklands up the hill to the Hall. I sat down on the floor, took up my pencil and began to sketch out four faces, the paper balancing on my knee. But only one of them was a living face, and I wondered how quickly she would see this.

They were in a boat thrown up and away by high waves. The boat had been ripped from its mooring by an earthquake, torn away from the land. It went under the sea, coming up wrecked and ruined. Rubble and lumps of wood covered their bodies, but I could see one face quite clearly, the lone survivor. I knew she'd need to see his face to identify him. But it wasn't Alfie, it was her brother Daniel who had survived.

She watched as the picture formed.

'It's Alfie, isn't it? It's him that's gone? It was the first time I'd begged him not to go but it didn't stop him, made him even more determined if anything. Course Alfie went, promising me it would be the last time, taking our Daniel with him.' She bit her lip, as if to steady herself before carrying on.

'Didn't think about me, though he *said* it was for me, said it was all for our future, to set us on the right track. Couldn't turn down that lump of money. Said he'd come back and we'd get married. Well, he won't be coming back now, he isn't coming back, is he?'

'No, sorry.' I shook my head.

It would start with a tremor that would fracture the land and creep out to shake the sea and neither of us could stand in its way.

'But Daniel? That's him, isn't it, that's our Daniel. He'll come back home, won't he?'

I nodded.

She stood up getting ready to leave. Dog whined a little as he wagged his tail at her. She held the drawing in her hand and reached for the door, but then turned around again, handing the drawing back to me. She didn't need it; it wasn't something she was going to hold close to her chest or put in her pocket for later. This wasn't a view of her future she'd want to see. She put it down on the little table gently, as if she was saying goodbye to something, and tapped it with her finger. She smiled and said, 'Thank you,' again and then reached into her skirt pocket. She pulled out a small leather purse.

Dog got to his feet and stuck his snout in her hand, sniffing the purse. She rested her hand on his head. He sat back down at her feet, looking up at her hopefully.

I don't know if it was Dog's eyes or the way he started licking her hand from the top to bottom as if he were cleaning her, but something made her start crying. She didn't make a sound, it wasn't dramatic; it was silent and steady. Her tears fell straight off her face onto Dog's head, but he didn't stop. Dog put his large jaw in her hand and she held him there.

She put the purse in my hand. It was soft on the outside and hard in the middle. She wrapped both of her cold hands around mine and said, 'I hope this will do you some good.'

It wasn't heavy but there was something inside it, an odd shape, one I hadn't felt before. It was round, like a circle. And then she kissed me briefly on my cheek before stepping over Dog, who was blocking the open doorway as if he didn't want her to leave yet.

We watched her make her way up the garden path, past the fence, heading back into the village, back to work. Dog stood in the doorway watching her, never taking his eyes off her until she'd gone out of sight. I wished I could have shown her something better, drawn her something kinder.

But *I* cannot tell a lie. I *cannot* tell a lie. I cannot tell a *lie*.

CHAPTER 11
NOAH

'What you looking for?' I ask her and take a swig of lukewarm juice. Beth has stopped in the middle of the river path and is searching in the depths of her bag. She pauses, passes me her water bottle to hold and carries on rummaging.

'My keys. I can't find my house keys and Mum and Dad will still be in surgery. I thought I'd put my key ring in the zippy bit, I usually do. Oh God, Mum's going to kill me. Look, my key ring's bust.' She attempts a smile but looks fed up with herself as she throws the broken key ring back into her bag.

'I'm already on my third set of house keys this year.' She puts everything else back in her bag then slings it over her shoulder. I pass her water back and we carry on walking along the river path, searching for the coolness of the shade made by the trees.

'So … what do you want to do now then? We could go back to mine if you want?' I stop in front of a bench. She sits down, dropping her bag on the ground again. I don't really want to sit down. The sun is making me feel tired. I want to keep going, keep moving and talking and walking.

'No, it's too hot to stay out and we've got to sort our photos out for the History project. It's next week, you know, and I haven't even seen your photos yet. I hope they are better than my kingfisher nests! Hey, I meant to say earlier … it's film night tonight, you know. Mum's cooking, which you definitely don't want to miss out on. She always makes way too much, so you can stay if you like?' she asks, not looking at me.

'Sure!' I answer far too quickly, all thoughts of an evening run with my dad taking a backseat.

'Anyway, we can still get in. We can walk through the field and see if the gate's unlocked, or climb over the fence. There's a spare key in the garage. Oh man, I feel like I'm having a sauna out here. Can we sit, just for a bit?' Beth points at me and gestures to the bench.

I throw my rucksack down next to her bag but I haven't done it up properly so half the stuff falls out. She reaches down to help me, handing me my text books, pencil case, my folder full of photos of her fish and the churchyard and empty crisp packets. She picks up my homework diary, which is already falling apart. She pulls at a page that is sticking out, hanging on by a thread. It is covered in green lines and shapes and symbols. She unfolds it and looks at it closely.

'What's this?' She holds the diary out to me and the honest answer is: I don't know. I don't remember drawing anything in my homework diary. I don't remember drawing anything in green pen either. I don't even have a green pen. I take it from her, feeling sick and unsure. Her face is straight and unsmiling.

I run my eyes over the drawing quickly, checking for anything dark and dangerous, anything of the usual sort. The relief nearly knocks me off my feet. I had been ready to run, ready to jump up and apologise or deny, dismiss, whatever it took to make things right. But it was just a drawing of her garden, of the summer-house with the open door and the tall daisies and chamomile. It was pretty good too.

'It's your garden. Not bad, hey? You can have it if you want,' I joke but she doesn't laugh. I feel cold all over. Prickles run up and down my arm like adrenalin but instead of a surge I feel the sharpness of something about to go sour.

'Why did you draw it? *When* did you draw it?' Her words come out clipped and crisp.

'Um, I don't know.' I look at my homework diary and can clearly see the drawing was on Monday, my first day of school, before I'd gone to her house.

'But how could you have drawn this on your first day if you hadn't even seen my garden? You hadn't even been back to my house yet. I don't understand.' She rubs her hand over her forehead as if to uncover something in her memory.

I don't know what to say. I run through my usual list of

excuses. I list reasonable explanations for things that are totally unreasonable, but none of them fit.

I don't want to lie, not to her, but there's no way I can tell her the truth either. She'd run a mile and I wouldn't blame her. I don't want her to leave me, I want her to stay. But there are some things I just can't tell anyone.

'*So?*' she prompts, arms folded, as she sits on the bench waiting, expecting some explanation that I just don't have. Where should I start? I knew it would come out sooner rather than later. It always did. I just wasn't sure how and when and that made me feel uncomfortable and out of control.

'Beth, did you ever play that game when you were little, a *let's pretend* game?' I begin, totally unsure where I am going with this question.

'*Huh*? What are you on about, Noah? What about the drawing?' She looks confused.

I close my homework diary and put it back in my rucksack. I stand up and kick it under the bench, out of sight.

'OK, so you're sitting in the back of the car, going on a trip somewhere, doesn't matter where, and you let your mind wander. You pretend *What if*? What if your parents are really someone else? Did you ever play that game?'

I perch on the edge of the bench, waiting for her reaction, hoping to get away with this random stream of thought.

'No. I don't get it. Can you stop going on about a stupid game and explain how you knew what my garden looked like? *Noah?*' Beth squints at me in the sunshine. This isn't going well but I'll have to carry on now.

'OK, basically I had a dream, not about you, nothing creepy like that, but I dreamt about your house, your back garden, and that's what I drew. It was just a dream, you know, *déjà vu* or something like that. I'd probably seen your house from Google maps or something when Mum was house-hunting. She made me look at stacks of Sible Hedingham properties on the internet. So you know, it went into my subconscious and then I had a dream about it. Pretty cool when you think about it?'

She's nodding, taking it in. I'm going to have to stop talking soon or I'll go too far and ruin it.

'Anyway, this game, right, you pretend that your mum and dad aren't who they say they are. They've lied to you all these years. They're criminals on the run, maybe bank robbers. Or they could be mass murderers for all you know. Now everything changes – your name could be fake, *your whole life is up in the air*. Everything you thought you knew is no more.'

She looks uncertain, both her eyes are open staring at me. And then she starts laughing, lovely and light and loud.

'You're weird, Noah. Anyone ever tell you that? You're really weird, but you know what – I like it. *I like you.*'

She shuts her mouth, as if she's said too much, and waves her hand at me to continue my silly story. She smiles, closes her eyes and leans back into the bench to enjoy the sun and let me entertain her with my strangeness. *She has no idea.*

'Now you have to decide if you are going to jump out of the car and run away from them and tell the police. Or are you going to stay with them, cos they're your mum and dad, right? They might be bad but they're all you know, these complete strangers. Can you trust them? After all they've done and said and lied about, is there any way you can trust them?' I ask her, testing the water waiting to see which way she'll jump. Whether I'll sink or swim.

'No idea, never played that game. My parents are GPs, Noah, so I'm pretty sure if they were up to something, leading secret double lives, I'd know about it. There's not much you can hide in a village, you know, you'd better get used to that!' She laughs easily at me, leaving the game behind like a casualty.

She didn't get it. I am not who I say I am. She didn't suspect a thing and why would she? Why should she, it's not like I'm ever going to tell her.

I played the stupid game every time we left another place, rewriting my past. I saw whatever town we left behind disintegrating in the rear-view mirror and I'd catch my mum's eye and I'd ask myself, 'Who the hell are you?' and more frighteningly, 'Who the hell am I?'

When we get to the fence the gate is locked. I cup my hands out and give her a leg up. She swings over the fence easily.

'There's a key in the garage, wait here till I get it? I'll go in through the back door and give you a shout when it's open.' She dumps her bag at my feet, walking off down the long garden towards the garage.

I stop at the edge of the hut finding a bit of shade from the roof. I can still smell mint in the air from where I fell earlier. The door is open again. I wonder if it might be cooler inside or like a greenhouse. I collapse onto one of the rickety chairs, but jump straight back up. I hear something moving, rustling behind me, a sound like an echo. I look down at the chair and see something small and gold shining in the sunlight. It is sharp – that's what I sat on. As I pick it up, a wind blows the door open.

'*Noah!* I've been calling you for ages, what are you doing? What's that?' She is out of breath. 'Didn't you hear me shouting?'

I shake my head. I hadn't heard her at all. I hadn't heard anything but whispering and the wind. I look down at my hand. I am holding a small gold key. Beth looks up at me with a question on her face and then back at my hand.

'That's *my* key. That's my front door key. Where did you find it?' Her questions are quick and fast and her voice sounds sharp.

'It was on the chair. I just sat on it!' I try to make a joke, not sure why the room is full of tension and secrets and not enough air.

'Really? Well, how did it get in here? I mean, how did *you* find it?' She keeps asking the same question as she takes the key from me.

'I just told you. It was on the chair. I came in here to get out of the sun.' I repeat myself, sticking to the facts.

'OK.' The tiny word falls out of her mouth, as if she doesn't trust it, herself or me. We stand in silence not looking at each other. Eventually she speaks.

'Well, cheers for finding it, I guess. Maybe I should get a new key ring, clearly this one is battered, key's always falling off. Did you bring your photos of the fish? We need to put our stuff together before we write our talk.' Her voice babbles on like a brook, just like normal, and all the volume returns to the room.

'I brought some of my photos but they're not that good. Your fish move so quickly it's hard to get a decent shot that's not blurred. I've started my bit of the talk too.' I copy her, speaking as quickly and loudly as I can, wanting to drown out my own voice trapped in my head.

'OK, let's go and get a drink and something to eat first and then we can put it all together. And after that I'll show you my Tim Burton film collection. It's not going to be as impressive as yours by the sounds of it, but at least I have a copy of *Big Fish*!' She shoves my chest with her hot hands and then pulls me out of the hut. I let go of one of

67

her hands but keep the other one for myself, as we walk slowly down her long garden to the house.

When I get home later that evening, I make myself a peanut butter sandwich with the thick ends of the loaf and sit down at the table opposite Mum and Dad. Mum quizzes me about my night straight away.

'Did you have a good time? What film did you watch?' She fiddles with the base of her wine glass as Dad tops it up.

'*Big Fish,*' I reply between mouthfuls.

'Sounds good. I haven't seen that one though, who's in that?' Dad asks, taking a small sip of his drink. He has red wine-stained lips and looks very chilled out.

'Um, don't know.' I answer. I'm not bothered by celebrities or actors, just the story.

'What are Beth's parents like? What kind of house have they got?' Mum asks, unable to stop herself. Dad and I start laughing at the same time.

'What? *What?* I'm just showing an interest.' She looks a bit cross so we both stop laughing.

'They're nice, you know, normal. They live in the Manor House. Umm … they're both GPs and run the surgery together, he's called Simon and she's called Rebecca. Beth looks just like her mum.' I struggle to think of anymore to say about them. Parents are just parents.

'Right. I've not met either of them yet. I should go and

register us with the surgery, shouldn't I.' She gives my dad a challenging look. He carries on sipping his wine.

'Did you get your History homework done, mate, or were you too busy with other things?' Dad changes the subject before Mum's next question can follow, winking at me.

'Yes, Dad, we got our homework done. We've got enough photos now. I'm going to paste them onto the boards tomorrow. The talk's on Wednesday so I need to practise,' I mumble, crumbs falling out of my mouth.

I point at his wine. 'No run tonight then, Dad? Thought we might get a late one in now its finally cooled down?'

'Sorry, mate, I was ready earlier but you were out on your date! *Just kidding, just kidding.* But seriously I'm wiped out now. How about an early morning one? I've got nothing on tomorrow or Sunday so I'm all yours, mate.' He spreads his massive arms wide, nearly wacking Mum in the back of her head.

'Right, well, let's see how your head is first before you go making him any promises about crack of dawn runs, Daniel.' Mum laughs as she moves the nearly empty bottle of red away from Dad. There's garlic bread in a bowl in the middle of the table. I grab a slice before pushing my chair back.

'I'll leave you to it. I'm going to go do my English homework,' I tell them.

'Have you started rereading it yet, the Dickens? I know you've read it before but I think you should read it again, you've probably forgotten a lot of it,' Mum suggests softly.

'I've read a few chapters. I'll go up and read some more now.' I walk towards the door.

'Noah, I'll be ready at 7 for a run, I promise. You up for it, ready to take on the pacemaker?' Dad asks pointing at me.

'Sure.'

'Night, mate.' Dad raises his glass to me and takes a sip. Mum smiles and blows me a kiss. I can hear them chatting as I climb the stairs and shut my bedroom door.

I take out my book, lie on my bed and try to fill my head full with Dickens's words about Pip, Estella, Miss Havisham and Magwitch, so there won't be any room for my own and it works for a little bit. But when Mrs Joe Gargery describes Pip as trouble and goes on to list all the things Pip has been guilty of and 'all the high places he had tumbled from and tumbled into and all the times she had wished him [Pip] in his grave,' it feels way too close to me. I throw the book across the room. I will my brain to hide my own guilt, but it is already on autopilot, playing another scene that I can't delete.

It had been my first parents' evening and I was proud and shiny in my new uniform, my jumper hiding the pen mark I'd got on my white top that afternoon.

'Sit down please, Mr and Mrs Saunders, Noah.' Mrs Games gestured to the chairs in front of her desk. My dad folded himself down and tried to perch on the edge of the chair. I thought he might fall off and had to squash down a giggle. Mrs Games had some exercise books set out in front of her. She started talking to my parents. I tuned her voice out as I looked around the room that was familiar but strange, empty of my friends and the noise and chatter that filled it up during the day. When I turned back around, Mrs Games had stopped talking and Mum and Dad sat in silence. My exercise books had been pushed to one side and on the table were two large drawings. I knew they were mine because I'd written my name proudly in big letters at the bottom, next to a shaky number 5. It had been my birthday the day before and I was practising writing my new number everywhere.

'Noah, what is this?' my dad asked, his voice low and quiet. I looked at the first picture and saw a beautiful mermaid underwater, her long white hair trailing after her. We'd read *The Little Mermaid* by a man with a long name and I'd tried to get the sea to be cornflower blue, but it had gone over the mermaid's face, which was annoying because it looked as if the water was squashing her face down. I had to draw her eyes closed because I couldn't do open ones yet.

Dad didn't look very impressed. Mum picked up the next picture and asked, 'Did you draw this one too, Noah?'

I looked at it and nodded. I'd spilled my red paint pot over the rocks I'd been drawing and it was really messy. My red fingerprints had gone all over the page, looking like I had cut myself, splashing drops of blood. The picture looked like a splodgy battle scene. I thought I'd stuffed both of them in the bin but Mrs Games must have taken them out. She was holding them out to my parents with her cross look and when she started speaking she used her indoor voice.

'As you can see, these are quite disturbing. I notice that Noah did try to throw them away, but I was emptying the bin and all the red caught my eye. You can see why we are concerned,' Mrs Games was saying, as if she enjoyed telling tales on me. My parents were nodding and thanking her. I didn't understand what for, she was showing them bad drawings. Why wasn't she showing them all the good ones I did of the starfish at the bottom of the sea or the pretty island I drew for the mermaid to live on? She had put those up on the display wall and stuck a gold star on them. I didn't like Mrs Games anymore, she was mean, but it didn't matter because that was my last parents' evening with Mrs Games.

CHAPTER 12
BLAZE

'I saw you. I saw you yesterday with that servant girl from the Hall on the hill. *Jenny White!* I saw you *touching* her and then I saw her hold your hands, her no better than she should be and … *you!* Did she give you something? Did she put something in your hands? I thought I saw her kiss you, but that can't be right, can it?' Emilia barged into my hut and stood over me, hands on hips waiting.

I didn't say anything. I'd heard her slam through the gate mumbling under her breath. I could feel the rage rolling off her like heat waves. I knew I'd done nothing wrong, but I wished there had been the time to pack my things away. I wished there had been just enough time to grab my box and hide what I'd been drawing.

'And I've seen the others, it's like some summer madness, all those lovesick puppies bounding in and out, your door opening and closing. I've seen silly skirts coming in empty and leaving with pockets full of pictures to match their stupid smiles. I've been watching you.' She pointed at me with her long thin finger, shaking with anger. I wondered what she'd seen and where she'd been spying from.

'And what did any of them ever do for you in return, eh? I bring you clothes, I bring you food and my company and what do I get out of the bargain?' She seemed to have forgotten the many vials of medicine I had made her.

'Well, your face has cleared, hasn't it? And your hands are healing really well, so my herbs must be helping you. Aren't they? I can always stop bringing you the vials if they are no good.' I left the threat hanging in the air, but she chose to ignore me, moving across to my little table, snatching up a piece of paper. And then everything else was forgotten, everything forgiven.

'What's this, lovey? What've you been drawing now, you clever thing?' she asked, her breath coming quickly. She looked excited, her eyes were sparkling and there was a thin smile forming on her now clear and pretty face.

'Is this me?' She looked hopeful.

'No, sorry, it's not you, Emilia,' I replied, hesitating, choosing my words as carefully as I could. I wished I could say, 'Yes, this is your future, that's your fate there outside the church with the flowers and the bells ringing and everyone come smiling to see you.' But it would have been a lie. My life would be a lot easier if I could lie but the words never flowed; they staggered about me falling in a heap. And the truth always came scuttling out in the end, like a black beetle.

'But why not? How do you know? This could be me; this could be me and Henry. You don't know everything.

Ha! How can you? You can't even speak English properly. You're just a boy, aren't you; after all's said and done you are just a *stupid runaway boy,*' she spat out.

'Then why do you come back, if I'm just a stupid boy?' I challenged and again she ignored me, carrying on her rant.

'You can't even write, for God's sake! I don't know even what I am doing here with you, a *foreigner.* If he ever found out, well, I just don't know what Henry'd do.' She began to pace, which was a challenge in the small space. Her bright yellow hair was falling out of the tight bun she wore. She kept grabbing bits of hair, forcing it behind her ears. Her skirts swished back and forth as she twitched and turned and I knew something was building, something was coming which would force me into a corner.

'Henry might feel it was his duty to help you out of this situation, lovey, set you on the right path as any good Christian man would. He knows a few people you see, a few Guardians who might be interested in your welfare. But there's no need to worry about that just yet, this can be our little secret, can't it. Haven't I kept you here all this time, tucked away in this hut? So many secrets hidden away down here at the bottom of this garden, aren't there, and you the biggest one of all.' Emilia glowered at me, holding my history over my head like an axe.

She knew everything; she had told me why they sent my mother away, told me why no one would come and see me down the Manor House path, told me why I had to hide from words like witch and workhouse and gipsy.

'Draw me now. Put that one away, whichever silly girl this one's for. Don't waste your time on strangers. Draw a friend's future instead. I have to know ... no, I *need* to know. Please? I'll bring you something good, something nice; make it worth your while, lovey?' she crooned in a light voice, as if asking a small favour.

'No,' I told her, standing my ground.

Her face closed in like the weather on a stormy night.

'Do it now or I'll tell. *Do it now* or I'll make you stop. I can put an end to you! I can finish all of this.' Emilia pushed me back down onto my stool and stood over me, keeping a bony hand on my shoulder. I sighed loudly, deciding not to fight her, not yet. I held my pencil, wondering what to do, what to draw. What could I show her that would just make her go away? I'd drawn her so many pictures, but none of them showed her what she wanted, so she ripped them up, threw them on my little fire and asked for more – always wanting more.

She pushed the thin paper towards me and it crackled and crunched. I smoothed it out flat with one hand and began drawing with the other. I had one thing left I could show her before she realised what the lines meant.

One more small delay.

I began to sketch circles, wrapping around something, over and over. Thick circles made of steel or metal that closed and didn't open. The circles went around and around and around, binding something forever.

Sealing it like a ring.

'Rings! *Wedding rings!* At last, I knew you could do it. I knew you could show me the right way if you just tried hard enough.' She sounded happy, as she patted me on the shoulder and smiled brightly at me.

'Ah, so you are a little fortune teller after all. I knew you'd see my future one day, mine and Henry Hall's.' She tore the paper out from under me and folded it carefully, placing it into her pocket. She rested her hand over it, as if to keep it safe.

'You've made my day, lovey. I'm looking forward to coming back and seeing even more next time.' She winked at me as if we were friends and left me with a spiky smile. Once this picture showed its dark self to her, she'd be back, without the smile, and then the storm would break.

CHAPTER 13
NOAH

'We're going to Broaks Wood tonight,' I whisper, pretending to make notes in my exercise book. I place my copy of *Great Expectations* in front of my face like a shield.

'Going for a run?' Beth asks.

'No, not tonight. Dad wants to take photos. There's a thing on, a walk with bats, it's run by the Essex bats group.' I look up to check where Mrs Ashwell is in the room. I don't want her to hear us and ask what we're talking about. She's really into sharing class conversations to embarrass us. She likes repeating what we've said in a loud sarcastic voice. The more time I spend in her classroom, the more she reminds me of Pip's sister, the dreaded Mrs Joe Gargery.

'Oh. Sounds good, if you like that sort of thing, I mean.' She sounds less than convinced with my plan. I have to give her something more.

'Why don't you come with us? Ask your mum. Everyone's meeting in the car park at 7.30pm? Come with *me*?' I ask as everyone starts to pack away, anticipating the bell. I want her to say yes. I need to ask her to do something, go somewhere with me other than her house or down to the river. I want us to go out, not on a date, but yeah, on a date, but I don't quite have the bottle for that yet. I need to work up to it.

'Not sure. Maybe. Anyway, I haven't finished *Great Expectations* yet. Pip has just begged Joe to forgive him. I completely love Joe Gargery, he's easily my favourite character. I know he's going to make things right for Pip, even though Pip has been so rude to him. I'll text you later if I'm coming.' She folds down the page she's on and puts the book in her bag as the bell rings. No one moves until Mrs Ashwell dismisses us.

'Beth, hang on, I've got something for you,' I call her back as she sets off up the corridor to her piano lesson. I reach into my rucksack, pulling out a paper bag with daisies all over it. I pass it to her quickly and try to look casual.

'What's this?'

'Open it and see,' I tell her smiling, hoping she'll like it.

She folds back the paper bag and peers in. Her face changes straight away and I wonder what she'd been expecting. She pulls the key ring out. It is a hand-carved wooden treble clef. It's a fairly largish one so hopefully she won't lose it or break it.

'I love it! It's lovely, *totally me*. Thanks, Noah.' She moves towards me in the busy corridor, but then stops before she reaches me. I thought she might have been about to kiss me. Instead she strokes the soft wood and then puts the key ring back in the paper bag, holding it closely to her chest. I don't know what she's thinking or what to say. She looks like she wants to leave, but at the same time I can tell she's pleased. It is way too confusing to work out what she's thinking, so I give up.

'So, I'll see you later then?' I ask shoving my rucksack onto my shoulder. She shrugs her shoulders, smiles, then runs off up the corridor, bumping into Eva and Georgia who have been watching and waiting. Eva holds out her hand, says something and then Beth reluctantly shows her the key ring. I turn away. I don't need to see the girls' reaction and the teasing that'll probably follow.

I wait for her later but she doesn't come. I'll have to do better next time, offer her something more than a bat walk in the dark, it isn't exactly difficult to see why she turned me down. Dad and I meet everyone in the car park. It's that in-between time, when the sun is still out, still hanging on low in the sky, not quite willing to give up its spot to the moon and the stars. It is my favourite time of day as no one really seems to know where they are – dusk, soft and suggestive, said in a whisper. *Twilight*.

'Did you get that book finished?' Dad asks as we walked along the riverside to Alderford Mill. Everyone's eyes are searching and scanning the sky, hoping for a spotting.

'Yep. I'd forgotten some of it so Mum was probably right,' I reply, looking up as the trees form a tunnel over our heads.

'She usually is, mate,' Dad jokes as we walked along together.

'"Ask no questions, and you'll be told no lies,"' Dad bursts out, his voice loud and out of place on the quiet walk. He looks pleased with himself. 'I read it last year when your mum did that evening class at the old college. She kept going on about it so much, I had to see what the fuss was about.' He waits for me to say something.

'Yep.' I want to be interesting and to talk to Dad about books and phrases and language, anything but myself. Of all the quotes he could have picked, that one was the worst. I look at him to see if it is a dig, if he's trying to make a point, if he realises how close to the mark he is. But I am way off course, his face is open. He tries hard to start up another conversation with me and I have to say something; I don't want him to think this is a waste of time, that spending time with me is dull and boring.

'"The broken heart. You think you will die, but you just keep living, day after day after terrible day,"' I quote back. I find it easy to remember things like quotes, not for long but they usually stay in my head long enough to use at school in a test or right now when I want to say something but don't have the right words. As soon as they are out of my mouth I realise these aren't the right words either.

Dad doesn't nod this time. This isn't the conversation he meant us to have. This is the conversation we usually avoid. He looks sad as he opens his mouth to say something, but the woman starts her talk and everyone stops walking to listen.

'Those sounds you can hear, the calling and singing, are nightingales. There can be as many as twenty-five males in the air. They're quite a small bird, about the size of a robin, but less colourful. We normally see them around May, but due to the heat there are still plenty of them about.'

She continues walking and talking and we all follow at a slow pace. The nightingales are making high-pitched sounds, twittering and singing to one another, trilling and whistling. It's very odd, like listening to a toy bird. I feel anonymous amongst this group of people, in the almost dark. No one is interested in me. I don't have to think about what to do with my face, or how to hide the pictures in my head from showing through my eyes. I can just be me.

I see the first bat right by the alder tree. At least I feel like I'm the first one to see it. I hold my breath. It is dark brown and small, much smaller than I had expected. It swoops low over my head and then high again, skimming the trees, diving down towards the riverbed.

'There! That was a soprano pipistrelle. They are the commonest and most widespread of all British bat species. Can you see how fast and jerky he is in his flight pattern? Their aerial agility is quite magnificent. A single pipistrelle can consume up to 3,000 insects in one night!'

the woman tells us as her bat detector clicks away.

We look up, expecting to see the same bat again, but instead see several others, silhouetted against the dimming sky, all swooping and looping through the trees. It is as if they've been there the whole time watching us with amusement. Their wings are flexed so far apart; they almost look like hands, waving.

'They are looking for small insects to catch and eat on the wing,' the woman whispers as we gather together, watching and waiting. It looks like a chaotic dance at dusk.

'It's called aerial hawking, when they eat on the fly,' my dad shares with me. I nod, even though I didn't know this. I look up at Dad's face but it is hidden by his camera. 'We all have sad things happen to us, Noah. We all do. Sometimes accidents just happen, terrible as they are. Sometimes there's just no one to blame, especially not yourself, mate.'

Later, when we walk back along the river, I think about what he said. I know he meant it but I can't accept it. If I accept what he's saying, would that mean forgiveness? But the words he's offering like accident and tragedy are things that can't be helped, that couldn't have been stopped and this could. I could have stopped it. I should have saved her and so there is someone to blame, there'll always be someone to blame. Me.

I feel a blast of air on my neck, warm and damp. At the same time across the river a large dog barks sharply,

CHAPTER 14
BLAZE

I opened the purse the maid gave me and shook a ring into the palm of my hand. The shine on it was golden and rich, like nothing I'd ever seen before. Maman never wore a ring, said there was never the time and place for one with my father. Told me the chance was taken from them. The only jewellery she wore were the stones around her neck, which paled in comparison to the gem I held. But it was cold, hard and sharp, not soft and warm.

I didn't know what to do with it. I could see it was precious and perhaps old and certainly worth something. The inside of the circle was dull and worn with time as if it had rested on many different fingers over the years. I wondered who had worn it last and who would wear it next. I could sense it wasn't new. It felt weighty as it sat heavy in my hand, full of history. I clutched it, my fingers closing around it like a secret. I imagined the green glowing through my skin, lighting me up, like an emerald fire that could burn, marking me out as a thief.

I had only one person to ask, one person I could show this to and trust. My one *friend*. I gathered up my coat, hat and the drawstring purse. I pulled it tight and tucked it in my pocket. This time, *I* would find *her*. I would go to her and ask a favour and offer her something she couldn't say no to. This time I would walk through the gate, down the river path and into the village to find her.

She thought she owned me; that I would always owe her. Well, this ring would even the balance finally. She could sell it for me and take her share of the profits and then I'd be free. I could leave, following the river Couënon all the way back home.

Dog jumped up and followed me out, trotting happily behind me as I pushed the gate open. He could sense my excitement as we headed down the path towards the village and the Swan Inn. For the first time since Maman died, I felt happy as I clutched the purse in my pocket and held on to it like hope.

CHAPTER 15
NOAH

'And don't forget: if you don't get your letter signed, you can't go on the History trip. Eva, stop talking! Are you guys listening? Letters, take them home, get them signed, bring them back. OK?' Mr Bourne waves a letter around in the air trying to catch our attention, but the prospect of a trip to some old museum in Halstead isn't swinging it. We're all too nervous about our assessed talks to focus on letters home, especially me. I've got no idea how this is going to go, if this is the right thing to do, but it's too late now. I've put the photo boards up on easels at the front of the class, so there's no turning back. I shove my letter to the bottom of my rucksack and focus on my breathing. Beth is already getting up, shuffling her cue cards, gesturing at me to hurry up.

'For our village life project, Mr Bourne said we all had to take portraits of our community. Beth and I chose to focus on animals rather than people. We thought of the famous fish in the long pond at the Manor House. You might already know this, but if you don't, these fish are not ordinary fish. They're called shubunkins and have been in Sible Hedingham for as long as the Manor House has stood.' I pause, glad to have got the first bit of my talk over with. I step back to let Beth take over and read from her cue cards.

'Shubunkins are pond fish with a difference. They are little comets, shooting around the pond, giving off sparks of colour like moving rainbows. Rather than being orange and gold and a bit boring, shubunkins are blue and their colour comes from beneath their scales rather than from the light above, like your average goldfish. Shubunkins have a black and orange mottling set on a bluish pearly background that shimmers in the sunlight. These are not just goldfish swimming aimlessly round and round.'

She finishes and the rest of the class laugh, even Eva, who never seems to manage more than a fake laugh. I'm sure most of them had a goldfish at some point, maybe from the fairground carried home in a plastic bag. I wonder how long the average goldfish lasts once home, after money has changed hands. Beth nudges me, it's my turn again.

'When we took photos of the fish, we found it hard to capture their blend of colours, shapes and form. We tried digital photos, Polaroids and normal film. It was really difficult to get a decent photo that wasn't blurred or close up enough. We got there in the end though and have put them all together to try to show you how colourful these fish are … they look like a floating rainbow.' I run out of breath and stop talking.

Beth turns over the three big photo boards I'd put up on easels in front of the whiteboard. I'd placed Mr Bourne and the rest of the class at the back of the room. Some people gasp and then everyone moves nearer to get a better look. Mr Bourne rubs his stubbly chin thoughtfully, as Beth steps back to take it all in.

I hadn't shown her the end result, just told her to leave it to me and that I'd mount the photos on the boards. She stands next to me and from this position can see what the rest of the class can't, what I want only her to see.

There aren't any photographs on the three big boards, not a single one, but there are hundreds of 6 x 4 drawings of her tropically coloured fish. She can see now that I have replaced all our photos with drawings, *my drawings*. From a distance they look like photos, photos that almost move and *almost* come to life. She looks at me with her mouth open a tiny bit, but says nothing. I don't know if I've done the right thing, but it is too late to take them down. And finally I'm sick of hiding. I don't know whether to smile at her or not.

The silence in the classroom is going on for far too long. People are staring at us, beginning to whisper and giggle.

'It's your turn.' I remind her, gesturing to the row of faces all wondering if we've finished our talk or not.

Beth stumbles over the first few lines of her section on barn owls, but manages to keep going. While she reads from her last cue card, I take my photo boards down.

Some people had moved out of their seats and were getting too close. This was just for her, not for anyone else.

I knew Mr Bourne wanted to have a proper look. He stood up and started walking towards the front of the classroom, but Theo was getting up with Eva, ready to take centre stage. Mr Bourne had no choice. He sat back down as I turned all the boards over, leaving nothing to see but blank canvases.

After class, Beth finds me in the dinner hall. She starts talking as if we're in the middle of a conversation. I move my stuff out of her way and she throws herself into the seat next to me.

'Why didn't you show me before today? Where did you get all those drawings from? Why didn't you use our photos?' Each question is quickly followed by another, but if I'd shown her before, it would have backfired. I have to do it like this, in a crowded room with nowhere to hide, or I'll never have the nerve. I don't say anything as I finish off the last slice of pizza. I want to know what she's seen first, what she's understood. I'm not sure how this is going to go and I don't want to say too much. I want her to work it out.

'Did *you* draw the fish like that?' she asks, staring at me.

I nod, not trusting my voice.

'How did you make them look like photos? No one else guessed, they all thought it was the photos we'd taken together.' She looks around the dinner hall as if people might be listening in on our conversation. Eva, Theo, Jay, Sam and Georgia are all sitting at the next table but are too loud to hear us and too interested in the joke Harley is telling to eavesdrop on us, except Sam, who seems to be staring into space. Clearly Harley doesn't have a future as a stand-up comedian.

'Noah!' Beth snaps her fingers in front of me.

'I found these drawings in my bag and some more under my bed and they looked better than our photos,' I answer and then fill my mouth with the remains of my chips.

'What do you mean, you *found* the drawings? Why were they under your bed? Why would you put drawings under your bed?' She looks puzzled.

'I don't know. I don't remember drawing them. I must have shoved them under there.' I wonder whether this is a bad move, again, but it doesn't feel wrong. It feels different this time. She feels different.

'OK, but why did you make them look the way they did? They look weird, like they're see-through or something. That's definitely not what our photos looked like.'

She is hovering on the edges and now I don't know if I want her to see the truth. I don't want to scare her. I keep changing my mind, knowing how it will end, but torn all the same.

No one has ever made me want to do this. I know it's dangerous. I should step back, but all I can see is her in front of me, waiting for an answer, trusting me, asking me to tell her who I am. And I want to, so much.

'That's just how I drew them. That's just how it happened.' I stick as close to the truth as I can.

'What do you mean, how it happened?' She catches the end of my sentence and holds on to it. I wish I could stop what I've drawn from happening, but it is too late. I don't want to make her cry, even though it is not my fault this time. I'm just the messenger. She fills my silence with more and more questions.

'I still don't see why you couldn't have shown me, or told me what you were doing? Why all the mystery? Why keep it a secret?' She keeps on prodding and pushing.

'Because … because I wanted it to be a surprise,' I answer weakly. This isn't the kind of surprise people like. Surprise is totally the wrong word. This isn't going to plan, mostly because I don't have a decent plan to work from.

'So where are they then, your drawings? I want to see them properly now.' She looks at the table as if I'd have left them lying there, for everyone to see. I tore them off the photo boards and put them away in my locker as soon as people started leaving the classroom, as soon as I could get them out of sight.

'I've put them away.' I don't offer to get them or tell her where I've hidden them. I keep eating. Her eyes never leave me.

'Well, go and get them then,' she snaps. She is getting

fed up with this. She just wants to understand and for a reckless moment I want her to. I imagine jumping up on the table and shouting it out loud to the whole cafeteria, telling them all in one hit who I am, getting it over with.

But I don't want to have to say the words. I can't. Because she won't believe me, of course she won't. I've been totally stupid. No one would believe this. I would sound like a liar, like a crazy stupid liar. So instead of any truthful words, I say just one.

'No,' I whisper.

'*No*? What's going on here? Why are you being so strange? Is there something you're not telling me? Because you know you can trust me, don't you? You can tell me anything, Noah… What is it? What's wrong?' She puts her hand on my arm.

It is too much; she has no idea what she's promising me.

'Just drop it, Beth,' I say, backtracking wildly. I take a sip from my can. I can see myself pushing her away, forcing her to leave me, to hate me even. I can hear my voice sounding cold, edgy and closed. I know she'll blame me. I've made a total mess of this. But she'll see it later, when she gets home.

'Oh *nice*. Yep, OK, consider it dropped,' she replies, scowling at me as she gets up, leaves my table and goes to sit with Eva and Georgia. I watch her pretending to join in with her back to me.

Eva's eyes stay on me as Harley reaches the punchline of his crappy joke. She doesn't laugh once.

I get a text from Beth at 9pm. I've been waiting for it since I got in from school. I thought she might ring me or just turn up at the door, so every time the phone rang I hoped. I wanted to get it over with. I imagined all the things she'd say, all the names she'd call me as I stood in the window of the lounge, waiting for the doorbell to ring, ready to run to let her in, to try to explain. But nothing happened all evening.

I'd told Mum and Dad I had homework to do. I sat at my desk surrounded by more drawings of her fish, all those upside-down animals. My phone vibrated across the desk.

12 of them are dead. Dead! There's only 8 left. What the hell, Noah?

I reply, my fingers flying over the letters.

Sorry. I'm so sorry. Can I ring you? Please?

Nothing. I knew she'd be angry with me but this silence was worse than her screaming down the phone. I decide to chance it. I look at my clock. 9:13. I'll call her and if she doesn't answer quickly, I'll cut it.

'*What the hell do you want?*' She answers on the third ring.

'I'm sorry. I didn't do it. I mean, it wasn't me. Your fish, it wasn't my fault.'

I'd spent all evening thinking about what I'd say, how I'd phrase it, how much I'd tell her, but now that she is on the phone, listening silently to me, I have no idea what to say.

'*Beth*?' I must sound desperate because she finally answers.

'Well, of course it wasn't your fault, you idiot. What a weird thing to say! Obviously it wasn't you. But you drew a lot of them like that – *floating*. That's how I found them, the ones that didn't make it. But how did you know so many of them would die? How could you have known?' Her voice peters out and I pause, waiting to see if she'll say more, if she'll make the connection. Terrified she will join the dots.

'So … you're OK with me then? You're not mad at me? You know, for drawing them.' I avoid her question.

'I said how did you know they'd die?' she repeats, not willing to let it drop.

'I don't know. That's just how I drew them, but I promise you I don't know.' It is the truth, sort of, well, a version of it anyway.

'It was just too hot for them, that's all. Maybe I should have thought, should have bought them in, put them in the tank or something. But they've been alright so far this summer. Oh I don't know. Dad says it happens; this heatwave isn't what we're used to. He said they've had loads of people in the surgery with heatstroke and heat rash, mostly old people. Mum had to send a baby to Halstead Hospital today, to be put on a drip, you know, for dehydration.' She pauses. I don't say anything, not sure whether she really believes what she was saying or is trying to talk herself into it.

'I should have looked after them better; it's my fault, not yours. I just feel bad, you know. There's supposed to be shubunkins at the Manor House and now I've let everyone down, I've messed up history.' She keeps talking, going on and on, her voice up and down and changing, starting slow then going fast. I can't keep up with her and her different tones.

'Beth? Beth, you haven't done anything wrong. There are still lots of fish left. They'll mate and there'll be more and the tradition will carry on. You haven't done anything bad.' I have to get her to see that this isn't her fault.

'You don't get it. Dad said we are the guardians, we're supposed to take care of things and I've messed it all up now. The fish were my responsibility,' she whispers down the phone. 'I shouldn't be on the phone. I've got to go … I've told them I'll be there tonight. Oh God, I don't know what I'm doing. Look I'm going; I've said I'll meet them down there. Bye.'

And then the phone goes dead and I'm left clueless. I couldn't hear half of what she was saying, but none of it is her fault; she hasn't done a single thing wrong.

But it isn't my fault either. I have to keep telling myself

that. I didn't make her fish die. I just knew they would. I'd drawn their dead bodies floating up to the surface before it happened. Before it happened. *Before.* And I need her to see it. I need her to know who I really am.

I just want someone to know.

The first time I drew the future, it happened too fast. I don't allow myself to think about that anymore, although I have no control over the nightmares. But after that I got it, I got what was happening, and I started to feel the warning signs. Then I could slow it down, I could watch it happen. I could pause it and turn the images around, upside down, back to front. I drew with my pencil, crayons, felts, paint, collages, anything I could get my hands on. I used old shopping lists, bank statements, empty envelopes, Post-its, school letters, diaries, colouring-in books and magazines, filling them all with pictures, images and drawings. I'd empty out the contents of my head onto paper, but it kept filling back up inside, brimming over.

Sometimes I used to watch and wait with a little smile on my face, knowing what was around the corner. I'd just about stop myself from singing out, 'I told you so.' Other times I'd run and hide. I'd bury my head under my covers and pillows and hope and wait. But I never stopped anything from happening by hiding or crying.

I've sat and drawn flowers, trees, cats, dogs, beaches and rainbows. I've drawn innocent people with light smiling faces holding hands. I've drawn islands in the sea hovering under a canopy of a stars, and this works for a time.

Then the unprogrammed drawing starts, the nightmares skulk in and get on the pages, spreading inky messages and threats. I destroy them, but find them again later, at the back of a wardrobe, in a chest of drawers, stuffed, torn, ripped apart, only to be repeated in colour, up close and magnified until I can see the picture without looking. It doesn't stop until I see it underneath my eyelids. No matter how tightly I close them, I see it all.

But she wasn't ready to see what I was trying to show her. Who would be? I thought she'd get it. I didn't think she'd do this: hide from what I'd shown her in those postcard images.

CHAPTER 16
BLAZE

She called to me, merrily waving from the half-open stable door of the kitchens.

The ring the sailor's fiancée had given me in her purse would save me. I'd need to buy some decent clothes first – if I had clothes I could look the same as the rest of them. With the money, I could head for the coast, I just needed to find someone to take me. And Dog of course. I could go back over the water to Maman's family. I just had to find them. I could follow the River Couesno and find the Ambroise women. If Emilia sold it for me, everything could change. I knew she'd want something for it, some coin for herself, but there'd be enough left, more than enough left for me. I'd never seen such a pretty ring, such a beautiful gem, not like my plain stones.

'What is it, lovey? Haven't seen you down here in a good while.' She called me over as if we were long-lost friends reunited at last, as if the sight of Dog and me in the village amused her.

'I have a proposition for you,' I said proudly, taking care with the adult word, but she laughed coarsely at me.

'Have you now? Well, aren't you just like the rest of

them! *Men*, you're always needing or wanting something or other.' She prodded me with her bony finger, laughing at her own joke.

I moved away from her and reached into my coat pocket, pulling out the drawstring purse. She breathed in sharply and rubbed her hand on her skirt. Her fingertips left a greasy stain on her clothes and I didn't want to put the beautiful stone in her slimy hands. She smelled of meat and animal fat. She felt me pause and laughed, wiping her nose on the back of her hand. It was red and I could see the broken veins under her skin. She held her hand out.

'Ah, ah,' I said, 'not yet,' using her own tactics against her. 'I need your word first. Your word that you'll sell this for me.'

Her eyes narrowed.

'Well, you haven't got anyone else to turn to, have you, lovey, so whatever it is, hand it over to your good friend Emilia,' she snapped.

'Your word,' I insisted. 'Then I'll show you what you've been asking to see,' I added, playing my best card last.

She stopped to look around, making sure no one else was listening.

'Alright then.' She pushed the bottom of the stable door open, stepping out and hovering excitedly in front of me. I shook the ring out of the purse. It dropped into the palm of my hand.

'Well, well, that's a pretty gem, I'm sure. Where'd you get that then, boy? Who gave you this?' she asked.

'It doesn't matter,' I replied, not wanting to give her anything.

'Let's have a proper look.' She held out her hand and didn't move it away from my face until I placed the gold ring on her flat palm.

'Emerald, gold band, proper gold this is. It's an engagement ring see. Of course you see, don't you, tucked away in that little hut, you close your eyes and see it all before the rest of us have even woken up and greeted the day.' She was talking to me, but her wide eyes didn't leave the ring, not once.

'This is what you drew for me, isn't it, you little gem. You drew those rings round and round and round and now here it is, in my hand. It's beautiful, that's what it is.'

She took the ring, clasping it tightly in her dirty hand, walked back through the stable doors and left me standing there empty-handed. I should never ever have given it to her. But then she came back with someone else.

Dog moved closer to me, pushing his head and shoulders against my thigh.

'Henry here will take this off your hands,' she said. 'He knows what to do with it. We'll give you something for it o'course, see you right. Won't we, Hen?' She nudged Henry in his ribs and he laughed. He towered over me, leaning out the stable door and clapped his thick, heavy hand on my shoulder.

'Don't you worry, boy. You're in safe hands here with me and her. We'll look after you, see if we don't. Come by in a few days and we'll have some coins for you, get you some new clothes and som'at to eat, eh? You look like you could do with a good scrub n'all!' He pointed at me, as if I were some kind of shame. I looked down at my coat, which had holes in showing the layers underneath. I nodded and ducked out from under his big hand and turned to walk away. Emilia wasn't finished with me yet though. She beckoned me back with her bony finger once Henry had gone back to serve in the taproom.

'Come here, come closer now, lovey, I won't bite! Now you know what'd happen if anyone caught you with this ring, or got to hear about it. So I'll help you out, once again, I'll do you another favour. Off you go, you get on back to your little hut, but make sure to come back and see your friends Emilia and Henry in a few days though, come back and see what we have for you.'

Her smile was stretched so thinly across her face that I could see her yellow teeth poking out under her lips. She smiled at me, swinging the empty purse back and forth in front of my face before tucking it away in her apron.

And then the smile dropped, replaced by a look of hunger, thin lips open wide ready to bite into something, chew it up and spit it out.

CHAPTER 17
NOAH

'Beth? Hi, what are you doing *here*?'

I open the door wider, balancing on the wooden ledge in my socks, tilting back and forth.

'I'm stuck on my English homework. Thought you might be able to help?' she asks.

Things have been different since the History talk. Three days passed and neither of us brought up what had happened with her fish. I hadn't gone back to her house because I didn't think she'd want me there. I'd used homework as an excuse and so had she.

I grab hold of her hand and pull her inside before she can change her mind. We stand there looking at one another, holding hands, then she shuts the front door. I lead her upstairs to my room. I close my bedroom door and she sits down on the end of my bed.

Beth is in my room. Beth is in my house. In my *room*. It's different at her house, it's fine there. Relaxed, safe, nothing to hide. But here? In *my* house? It feels like anything could happen.

I'd woken up that morning at my desk, my head lying on another picture of her. When I opened my eyes, the first thing I saw was Beth, crying. This wasn't the first day that had started with pictures of Beth crying. But I didn't know what had made her cry, or who. I hoped it wasn't me, but guessed it probably was, which was why I'd kept my distance these last few days.

'Anyway … so…' she starts and then stops. Awkwardness begins to cloud over us, a pressurised silence. I want to fill it, but don't know how. I want to say sorry again about her fish, but don't want to go back over what happened or who is to blame. I knew things would end with me feeling guilty – they always do. I stand in the middle of my room. Eventually I force myself to speak, to break the tension.

'What do you feel like doing?' I ask, trying to get back to normal.

I nod at the space next to her on my bed. She moves across to make room for me. I lean back against my headboard, which creaks and groans embarrassingly.

'I don't know. What do you want to do?' She looks around my room. I try to see what she might see: plain white walls covered in pictures by various artists; odd prints by Dali of melting clocks hanging off trees next to some strange loud ones with sharp notes of colour by Kandinsky. She pauses to look at the Van Gogh one, *Starry Night*, with its midnight skies rolling like waves, surrounded by spinning stars.

I'd drawn my own variations and pinned them around

the original, like constellations, but I didn't tell her this, I didn't want to draw attention to my own stars. I could see which one she liked the best: the one on the ceiling above my bed. It had caught her eye. I put my head back on the pillow, next to Beth's, and look at it with her – it is slow and gentle, warmth and tenderness running in waves down the back of a golden dress that sighs and shimmers as the couple cling on to one another.

'Who painted that one?' she asks. I look at the painting then at her and clear my throat.

'Gustav Klimt, an Austrian painter, my favourite. He said, "Whoever wants to know something about me should look carefully at my pictures."'

As I say it, I realise that's what I'd been trying to do, with her fish and the pictures. I wanted her to know me. But it was a mistake.

She is still pointing at the picture, waiting for an answer. I don't know what she's just asked so I keep talking.

'So … this one is of Klimt and Emilie his … lover. It's called *The Kiss*.'

I feel something hover between us, but I'm a moment too slow to catch it. I lean in towards her just as she pulls back, away from me, and jumps off the bed kicking her flip-flops off onto the floor. There is a beat of emptiness and then she starts talking, filling the silence with something completely different. It takes me a second or two to catch up.

'So did you get the English homework? I thought maybe we could do it? I mean, do the homework. Together.' She looks around for somewhere to work, a clear surface and seems shocked at how messy my desk is. It is covered in paper and drawings and pages torn from magazines like a collage.

'I didn't have a clue what Mrs Ashwell was going on about. Pip and symbols of justice and the role of guilt in the novel? I mean, he's innocent, isn't he, clearly? I've got the essay question and stuff in my bag.' She reaches across to her flip-flops, but there is no bag.

'I must have left it downstairs in the hallway. I'll go and get it, you clear that mess off there so we've got somewhere to work in this pit!'

She leaves my room. I jump up and rifle through all the pictures on my desk, trying to find the right one. I shove some of them into the top drawer, which is already pretty full. I ram more into the bin. As I spin around with another handful to hide under the bed, Beth comes back in and we collide in the small space. My drawings fly up into the air and land everywhere.

My hands are on her shoulders, where I'd steadied myself so I wouldn't crash into her. But now I can't take them away. It is like they are stuck. I pull her in to me and move my hands from her shoulders, down her back, pushing her forwards into my body. I can feel her against me and hear her breathing. Her hair smells of lemons, or something citrusy. She doesn't push me away this time, or try to move back, which I take as a good sign. I lean all the way down as she sweeps her hair out of her eyes, stands on her tiptoes and moves her mouth to mine. Her lips are hot and sweet and very soft. She tastes like strawberries. I nearly forget to breathe so, when she eventually pulls away my whole body feels like pins and needles, but in a good way. I rub the back of my neck which aches from stooping for so long. I'm not sure what to say to her.

'Sorry, I … I don't know what to say after that. *Wow!*' she says, pulling her hair back across her face again, smiling widely.

'Sorry, *sorry*.' I'm not sorry at all, but I don't know what she is thinking or feeling. I am feeling awesome, fabulous, amazing, on top of the world, totally epic – all the phrases I'd heard people say all the time, but never used myself before because they'd have felt fake. This is how I should have felt before, in other places with other girls, kissing. This is real, in this new room with this new girl, and it feels nothing like before.

'Are you OK?' I ask, needing to know what she is thinking.

'Yep, you have no idea how OK! That was so different to when…' She stops talking and laughs instead. She takes a step backwards and watches me for a second, then bends down to hide her face and her smile. She gathers up some of the paper off the floor. I want her to come back and kiss me some more, but don't have a clue how to make this happen. She carries on tidying up the mess while I wonder what to say next, what to do next and how to move things on.

'Is this your homework? It's in a right state and *oh* … oh?' she stutters as she takes in what she's holding. It is a drawing of her. The one I don't want her to see.

I'd found the first lot a few days ago under my bed and more this morning. The new one is much more detailed. I hadn't realised in the others that she was sitting at her piano, her fingers paused over the keys, hands hovering in mid-air. This new drawing was big and close up. You could even see the veins under the skin on her hands, each knuckle and line. Beth stares at it, taking it all in. In the drawing, tears had run down her face and were pooling in the dip at the bottom of her neck. It looked like she'd been crying for a while and hadn't wiped them away. In the picture, it was just her, sitting on her own, crying. I wanted to know why, to make it better.

'What is *this*? What-the-hell-*is*-this?' she hisses at me, too angry to shout. She shakes the drawing at me and then her body folds at the middle and she falls onto the floor. I stand over her. Heaviness settles in my stomach and pushes down on my shoulders, rooting me to the spot. I have nowhere to hide.

'It's a picture I drew of you.' I decide to stick to the truth.

Everything else I've tried is too complicated and doesn't work. Maybe the truth will make sense for once, not all of it but some of it.

'I can see that. I can see it's me, but why are *you* drawing it? Were you spying on me, Noah? Were you looking through the window last night watching me? *Oh my God!'* She draws herself away from me, tucking her legs and feet underneath her.

'No, no, no way. I'd never spy on you, *never*. I'm sorry, Beth, I'm so sorry. I wasn't watching you, I promise, I totally promise. I was out running with my dad. Why, what happened last night?' Now I am worried.

'How did you know about this unless you were watching me? How do I know you were with your dad?'

I shake my head and look wildly around my room for something I can do, something I can say to change what she is thinking. She's getting it all wrong. Getting me wrong.

'I drew it before last night. I drew loads of others like it days ago. I draw things, I keep trying to show you that, to tell you…'

I am making a mess of this. I walk around in circles trying to find the right words.

'Tell me *WHAT*? Stop walking around. Stop!' she shouts at me, not caring that my parents might hear.

'I draw the future.'

There. I said it. It is out. I'd tried showing her, I'd tried hinting at it, I'd tried making fun of it, but it was all a waste of time. She wasn't getting it. I didn't want to hide it from her, so I had to just stop and say it, just tell the truth and trust her, like she asked me to.

'*What?* What are you on about you *draw the future?* Noah, are you mad?' she shouts at me as she jumps up. She is looking at me as if I am a complete stranger. Her eyes flick over to the door and part of me wants to fling it open and let her escape and another part of me wants to stand in front of it and block the way out. But I don't want to scare her, not any more than I already have. I have to make sense of this for her. It is too late to do anything else now.

'The pictures of your fish I drew them before they died, didn't I? I drew that before it happened.' I move towards her.

'Yeah, but that's just coincidence. It was just too hot. Loads of animals have died in this heatwave. You can't make stuff happen, Noah, that's just not possible, not in the real world.' She shakes her head at me, as if I am dangerous.

'I *know* I can't make stuff happen, OK? I'm not saying I can. I never said I had any control over it!' I shout back at her, then stop myself. This isn't her fault.

'Sorry, sorry, I didn't mean to shout at you. Let me try and explain, Beth, please? I draw stuff before it happens. I always have. I don't know what's going on, but lately I'm drawing more of the future than I've ever drawn before.

It's all started changing, since I met you, I think. Since we moved here.'

I stop for a moment to try to slow down my thoughts. She nods at me, telling me to carry on, but doesn't come any closer.

'Lately if I throw a drawing away, I end up drawing it over and over and bigger and in more detail, like the ones of you playing the piano. I draw them and draw them until I know them off by heart. It feels like sitting down to watch a film but I don't seem to be able to pause it anymore, or press stop or rewind. It is out of my control. All I can do is watch it play out in front of me.'

I reach down to the floor and pass her a handful of scrunched up drawings – all of her at the piano, all from different angles. One in profile, another the back of her head with her long messy hair trailing down her back. Each one bigger and bolder, more colourful and more complicated than the previous one. Every possible angle.

She doesn't know what to do with them so she just holds them, standing there in the middle of my room.

'I was playing *Adagio for Strings*,' she says. 'It always makes me cry, even when nothing bad has happened. Mum and Dad were doing Friday evening surgery so I played, most of last night actually, once I'd got back. But the thought of someone watching me, the thought of *you* standing outside the window watching me play and cry is … horrible, Noah.'

She doesn't believe me. She thinks I've been prying at the window like some village idiot.

'What do you mean: even when nothing bad had happened? Do you mean the fish? I've said I'm sorry. I'll buy you some more if you like.'

She snaps up her head and shouts at me. 'It's not about the fish, for God's sake! I wasn't crying over the stupid fish OK? It was … I went out. I shouldn't have gone but they kept on asking me, daring me and you'd upset me – *yes about the bloody fish* – so I went. I met them down the graveyard.'

She flumps down onto the carpet, her hands in her lap as she moves her rings around and around on her fingers.

I hold my breath in really hard to stop myself from reaching down and shaking the story out of her. I have to know who's made her cry.

'They were playing KISS/CRUISE/MARRY. Harley gave me my options: him, Theo and you.' She stops, her voice cracking as she starts crying softly, her head down.

This is torture. I need her to spit it out, just tell me what's happened. I know the game – you have to say who you'd kiss, who you'd be stuck on a twelve-month cruise around the world with and who you'd marry. I sink down onto the carpet next to her. This time she doesn't move away.

'I said I'd go on a cruise with Harley, even though I never would, that I'd kiss Theo, which ended in Eva having a massive strop, and that I'd marry … that I'd *marry* you,' she splutters as she breathes in on a sob. I pull her forwards awkwardly and wrap my arms around her, feeling her body relax against me.

'So why did that make you cry?' I don't get what has upset her so much.

'Because Theo then grabbed me and kissed me really hard for ages. He stank of fags and I tried to push him off, but Eva said it was all my fault, that I'd led him on, that I was always flirting with him and Harley called me a … called me a tease. And then they all left me there in the graveyard on my own in the dark.'

I rock her back and forth, mumbling stupid things like it will be OK, it'll be alright. All the time thinking *she'd marry me, she'd marry me, she'd marry me!*

When I stop talking, she turns her face up towards me. I want to kiss her again to erase Theo's stale kiss from her lips. But I can't. I have to show her something first, the last drawing that I tried to hide. I can't hide anything else from her now. There is nothing – almost nothing – left to hide.

'I've already seen this. You showed me this before.' It is of her hut. And she is right, she's already seen it, but there's something neither of us had noticed, until now.

'Look through the door.' I push it back towards her.

'OK, yeah … what am I looking for?' She sniffs as she brings the large sheet up to her face.

'Look on the chair.' I'm not sure how she'll react, but I know I have to do this.

'My key!'

The realisation hits her.

'This is from before. You drew this before I even lost my key, didn't you? Did you know when you went in to the summer house that the key would be there? *Did you?*' She is shouting at me again. She's ripped the corner of the picture by holding it too tightly. She's back on her feet now.

'No. I didn't realise I'd drawn the key then. I didn't even notice it, not until after it happened, honestly.' I am being truthful, trying to be honest, but this time I stay on the floor, away from her.

'This is really creepy, Noah, *just creepy*. It's freaking me out. Maybe Eva was right about you, you're just too much. I need to go home. I don't want to be around you right now.'

I start to get up, holding out my hands to her.

'No, don't say anything, *don't touch me!*' She holds her hands up, as if to ward me off. The tears in her eyes push me back to the floor.

She takes the pictures with her, shoving them into her bag as she walks out of my bedroom. I watch her from my window, wishing I could call her back. I could run after her and say sorry, whatever it takes, but I know there are no words. Not for this. Sorry was never going to cover it.

CHAPTER 18
BLAZE

I stood outside The Swan waiting for one of them to come to the stable door. Dog refused to sit and stood next to me, hackles raised. He started pacing between me and the door, back and forth, back and forth. I didn't know how long it would take for one of them to notice me. Although people in the village kept their eyes on the ground when they walked past me, I knew I stood out. Women who had visited me in the past walked past nervously, arm in arm with men who looked over and around me like I was a bad smell. I could see the panic in their eyes as they recognised me, worried that I'd give them away. But I didn't. I didn't look in their eyes, I kept my gaze on the ground as I kicked at the dirt, my feet moving about too freely in my large boots.

They weren't coming, not today. I'd have to come back again tomorrow. I clicked my tongue at Dog, ready to leave, when she flung open the top door.

'Ah, someone said they'd seen you lingering out here. Like a bad penny. So what do you want now, eh?' she cried out, waving a sharp knife in one hand and a potato in the other. I stood and stared at her, lost.

'Come for some more food, have you? Come to ask for work?' she shouted out loud, as if she was talking to the whole village not just me. I frowned at her. She knew what I'd come for. She *told* me to come. I'd come for my share of the ring.

'Spit it out then. What is it? I haven't got all day to waste on the likes of you. I'm a busy woman see.' She scratched in her hair with dirty nails, encrusted with mud from the potatoes she was peeling. She hadn't opened the door. She wasn't stepping out to see me this time. She wouldn't look at me either, delivering all her lines to the air behind me.

'Money?' I asked. 'I gave you the ring,' I prompted her when she pretended to look confused.

'Ha, ha, ha! Now what would you be doing with a ring, eh? What would someone like you being doing with a ring? That's a good one that is, *funny that.*' She pointed at me with her knife and I saw it sparkling on her ring finger. She was wearing it. My ring!

'Talking of rings, I guess you must have heard my good news. I'm to be married. Henry asked me only the other day. Came as *such a surprise.* There now, just look at you! You look shocked, like you've seen a ghost. *Wasn't it something you'd forseen, boy?*' She whispered the last bit, taking care that no one should hear. She showed me the ring again.

She'd taken it. There wasn't going to be any fair price or exchange. Neither of them were going to see me right.

There wouldn't be any new clothes or boots that fit or a ticket to France.

She thought that's what I had drawn. She thought those rings, steel and metal, were emerald engagement rings and wedding bands. She had no idea what those circles really meant, but I'd make sure now – I'd make sure that she wore those circles forever, *till death do us part*.

'I've seen your future. I've seen what happens to you,' I hissed at her, making her jump, and then I laughed out loud as the smile fell off her face. She looked frightened of me for the first time, shutting the door, leaving me there with my empty pockets. Like an angry fool.

CHAPTER 19
NOAH

It's strange to be walking past the river on my own without Beth. She won't talk to me at school. She's not talking much to anyone. Eva and Georgia keep blanking her, Theo keeps winking at her, leaning up too close against her locker when she tries to open it, and Harley gives her nasty looks as if she's something less than him, which is a joke.

She says stuff, passes me worksheets and still sits with me for lunch, but it's like she's not really there. Like she can't relax around me or be herself anymore, and I don't know what to do about it.

I haven't got a clue how to fix this because it's never happened before. I've made fake friends, pretended, acting like I care about music and films that help me fit in. I've joined in with meaningless conversations and gossip, taking care to wear the right clothes and hang out in the right places. But I've never told anyone the truth before. Pretending was always easier, but this time I couldn't do it. I didn't want to. This time it felt real.

And I've messed it all up. I've wrecked it before it even really started, and I'm back to the plastic smiles, the cover-ups and empty conversations.

Eva and Georgia keep walking past her at break, around and around the yard, looking at her, making faces and comments, trying to flirt with me. I ignore them, which weirdly seems to make them try all the harder. When she comes back to me in English or History, it's like being friends with a ghost, a faded version of Beth, not the real thing. If I reach out my hand to touch her, she moves away. When she smiles at me it's like a shadow smile, not solid enough to stay for long.

I tried writing her a letter, apologising again, but everything I wrote seemed empty and never quite enough. So I screwed up my words and threw them away, only to find them the next morning covered in lines that aren't anything, drifting and discoloured. I find more scraps of paper, dripping with images that I can't make any sense of as they skim and skate across torn pages from my exercise books.

Now we talk around the edges, making conversation as if we've just met. She says things like, '*It'll blow over, it's just a phase, it'll pass,*' and maybe she's right, maybe next week they'll all be friends again, but what about her and me? I don't know how to repair whatever we were starting to have.

I pick her flowers in the field behind her house, oxeye daisies, wild poppies, dandelions and buttercups, anything bright I can get my hands on. I haven't got enough money to get her something from Daisy's the florists in the village, not that I'd go in there on my own anyway. I hoped she'd like wild flowers more than something grown in a greenhouse or polytunnel.

I've written another letter and this time I'm going to give it to her, or at least leave it for her to find. Not really a letter, more of a note to stick next to the flowers. I had one Klimt card left from a set Mum bought me for my birthday. It was *The Kiss*. I think I'd been saving it for a special occasion. I'll just leave them on the front doorstep and leg it, hoping she won't see me. I don't want to make her feel worse. I want her to look at the card and remember the kiss we'd had in my bedroom, before I trashed everything. I've been half-expecting her to give me back the key ring, but she hasn't yet.

I read the note again. They aren't my words. I borrowed them from our English lesson, but they say what I want to better than I can. Hopefully it will show her how much I want her to trust me again.

> 'Heaven knows we need never be ashamed of
> our tears, for they are rain upon the blinding
> dust of earth, overlying our hard hearts.'
> Pip says it better than me,
> Noah

I reach her front door, put the flowers on the step and place the card next to them, hoping she'll see them before her parents. She said earlier she couldn't walk home with me today because she needed to do her piano practice. I was sure it was an excuse, just another way to keep me at a safe distance. But through the open window I hear music. It must be the piece she's writing, that she's trying to get right. It is beautiful.

I can't move, I have to listen to her play, even if she sees me, even if it ruins the flowers and the note and all my good intentions. I sit on her doorstep and wait until the piece is finished, until the notes have stopped climbing and dipping, making me feel so many things.

I get a text from her just as I get back from my run with Dad. He smiles at me as I fling my dusty trainers off in the utility room then run upstairs to read it alone.

> Hey you. Those words were everything I needed to hear, the weeds aren't bad either. Walk home together after school tomorrow? Bx

I send my reply immediately.
Yes.

CHAPTER 20
BLAZE

A little after the sun went down, Dog started howling, the sound vibrating in his chest. He looked like a lone black wolf stood at the door with his nose in the air, throat strained as he made the painful sound. I packed most of my things away but kept my knife out, tucking it carefully into my coat pocket, ready and waiting.

She didn't knock. She came straight in despite Dog and his sharp teeth bared beneath his curled lip. She pointed at him, as he stood in her way, hackles raised making him look even bigger. My brave wolfhound.

'Get him out, get *that* out of here … if you want me to stay that is. The last thing I need is to be cooped up in here with that flea-ridden hound. *Filthy thing.*'

She pointed at Dog as if he were some kind of wild animal. I didn't want her to stay, but clicked my tongue at Dog and he closed his lip down over his large yellow teeth, bent his head low to the ground and slunk out, half in the doorway, half out.

She slammed the door, but his paws were in the way. Dog yelped and jumped back in pain, and I wanted to go to him, but she blocked my way, shaking her head to say *Stop. Do not move, do not take a step.* I stood still and waited.

'So I've bought something for you, lovey. Like I promised. One gift for another, that's right, isn't it, that's how things are between you and me. Fair is fair.' She smiled at me, but I knew I'd never trust her again. She was holding her basket close, sniffing the air in a theatrical manner. She took out a hot parcel which smelt like meat. She had the ring on and saw me looking at it. I wanted to rip it from her hand, but knew better. I needed to wait and watch for her next move.

'Ah, hope you don't mind, decided to hang on to it in the end. Henry liked it and once he realised it was an engagement ring, well, the seed was planted and, as they say, love blossomed. *Ha, ha ha!*' She shrugged as if all this was nothing to do with her. I didn't say a thing and she looked disappointed in me, as if she'd expected tears or rage.

I gave her neither.

'Well, you leave me in a bit of a bind. I had this lovely meat pie for you, seeing as how you enjoyed the last one so much, but I'm not sure if you deserve it yet. Not sure you've quite earned it.' She adjusted the basket, hooking it on her arm then opened the parcel, unwrapping the layers of muslin to reveal another pork pie, this one larger than the last. Steam was still coming off it and my mouth watered, despite my best efforts. I clamped my teeth together and bit down hard on my lip, not willing to show her any sign of weakness. The hut filled with the smell of pastry and my stomach gave me away, rumbling loudly. She made a tutting noise, as if to say, *What a shame you are.*

'Now, I didn't want to have to do this, but you've left me with little choice. You've two roads you can take here, you can do the right thing and take this lovely pie I made you, *mmm, smells good, doesn't it?* Show me what I've asked you, seeing as you know everything.' She held the pie out to me, just far enough away so I couldn't reach out and grab it from her and ram it into my mouth.

'Or we can make things harder for you, make things a bit more complicated. Is that what you'd like?'

She began wrapping the pie back up, sealing in the steam and the scent, then put it back in her basket. She waited for me to speak, twisting the ring round and round on her thinning finger. It kept catching the light coming in from the moon outside.

I said nothing.

I gave her nothing.

I stood there, waiting, waiting and watching her with my eyes wide open now. Wise to her and her schemes.

'Like that, is it? Well let's see now … if I told someone, perhaps a magistrate, that I found this engagement ring here in your little pit, well … you'd be doing hard labour before you could spit. Not that I'd wish that on my worst enemy, let alone a *friend*.' She stopped and examined her hand, holding the ring up, twisting it back and forth to admire it. Her hands had reduced in size. The medicine was working. She kept her eyes on the ring as she carried on talking.

'In fact, they might take such a person, a thief like that, straight off to the workhouse while they decide what to do with them.' Her voice caught in her throat when she saw my face. I was too slow to hide it – she'd seen my horror.

'*Oh dear.* Oh no, have we had a fright? Have we been having bad dreams about going back to the nasty big workhouse? Don't want to end up back in there, do you? Can't see that they'd let you escape a second time.'

I shook violently, trying to hide my fear and my memories, but she saw it, she knew it all. That was the problem, she knew everything. It was so hard to hide myself from her now because I'd trusted her before.

'You know just what it's like in there, don't you? I've heard tales, o'course I have, but I'll bet the reality is a far sight worse than the tallest tale.' She looked happy, as if she'd found something even better to think about than the ring.

'But if you were to give me what I want, to show me what I want, well, then I'd be happy to help you out. *Poor old soul that you are.* I'd be happy to let you have a few bottles from the taproom, a loaf or two every now and then, out of the kindness of my heart. Maybe a few more pies like this one. And I'd be happy to keep your secret, for a bit longer.'

She stopped to let me speak, waiting for me to say yes.

But I didn't.

I stood silent and steady, watching her.

'Show me! Come on now, just show me that things work out for us and be a good boy, eh, because you know where bad boys end up, don't you!' She made the last word '*bad*' sound so cold and the word '*good*' sounded wrong coming from her. She was anything but good. It was almost time to show her why, but not just yet. *She* could wait, for a change, let her stand there feeling lost and clueless for once.

She rubbed her hand over her forehead as if thinking things through, waiting for me to fill the silence, but I didn't give her a word, not a single sound. She snapped, just as I'd known she would.

'Well then, *that's that*. You've made a mistake this time. This is the last time I'll ask you nicely. I could have been good to you, I could have been so good. But you remember my words – this is what *you've* chosen.'

'Yes, this is what *I've* chosen,' I answered, enjoying the surprise and confusion on her face.

She swung around and threw herself out of the door, kicking Dog out of her way as she stormed towards the fence. She paused once, looking over her shoulder with a spark of fear in her face.

I stood in the doorway, Dog in front of me, and watched her break into a run all the way down the river path.

CHAPTER 21
NOAH

I wake up under my bed; my legs backed up against the wall, toes cramped and cold as if I've been out of bed for hours. Maybe I have. My arms and head are sticking out into the room; the rest of me is buried underneath paper.

I've been doing it again, drawing in my sleep instead of dreaming. I try to adjust to the early morning light to see what I've drawn. Faces are scattered across my floor. Cold, blue eyes look up at me. It's the same face again and again, as my vision blurs and then focuses. Each picture is from a different angle, a different time of day. In some I've zoomed in close on her pale face and her long yellow hair. In others I've caught her from a distance in the frame of her bedroom window, taking her tie off with a soft smile on her face. They are each like a film stuck on pause: one character, one scene jumping and flickering.

She is smiling in all of them, the smile she throws over her shoulder as she walks away. It isn't a nice smile. There is no fear, no guilt. She's *enjoying* it. She is pushing a small boy, her brother, out over the window ledge, her hands on his shoulders as she tilts his body back. I can't see his face, I haven't drawn it, but I know it's him. She has her school tie round his throat. I can imagine his terror as he looks down at the ground way below him. But I don't know when this is going to happen or how to stop it, and that panics me. The familiar fear rises like heat up my body reminding me of how useless I am, how slow to act, to think. I screw the picture of her face up in my hand, blocking it out. I've seen faces like this before, images that don't make sense, don't tell me enough about who and what and where and when. And when the picture finally starts to make sense, of course it's too late.

I gather up the papers. They crackle and crunch in the early morning quiet. I freeze, waiting for Mum or Dad to come barging in. I sit there with the evidence in my hands. But my door stays shut. I look at my clock – it is only 4am. They must be still asleep. I can take the drawings and shove them in the recycling bin outside the back door. I can cover her face with soggy cereal boxes and useless junk mail, bury her underneath egg cartons and free newspapers, getting rid of her and her stupid smile.

I scrunch the pictures up, folding, bending her eyes, false smiles and sharp fingernails. I creep downstairs, taking care not to let the kitchen door slam shut behind me. The back door is locked. It makes a clicking sound as I turn the key. The patio is cold and damp. If only I'd put on some socks. I can't leave a telling trail of wet footprints across the clean kitchen floor. I'll have to be quick and quiet. I hold the lid of the bin open with one hand and

CHAPTER 22
BLAZE

I lifted myself over the fence and out of the garden. The gate was stuck fast again, swollen in the heat. I headed for the river, my pocket heavy with the stone ring and the vial. I ran down the winding path, ducking under leafy ash trees that made tree tunnels over the water. I was soft and silent, alone, having left Dog sleeping under a rose bush, drowsy from the long heat of the day.

I'd gathered nettles yesterday and mixed in other herbs, binding them with river water into a lump. I kneaded the ball until it felt solid enough to use and then cooked it down in the pan over a small fire. Once it had cooled, I poured it into the glass jar. I pushed a cork into the top to seal it, taking care, I needed every drop.

Last night I left a new vial on the open windowsill of the kitchen, where she always kept my potions, swapping it for the one she usually had. She'd never know the difference, not until it was too late. If that new vial had done its job, then tonight would be the last time I'd see her. I'd never make her anything or try to heal her or help her again. But I'd have to be quick to replace it with the fresh one in my pocket, the one I normally made her. I'd have to be so quick.

131

As I neared the village, I slowed my pace, checking in my pocket for my knife. It was still there, next to the stone ring. The river was still and empty and the pathway up to the Swan Inn clear. I heard a nightingale starting up a song as I walked up to the outline of the stable door. I didn't need a lantern, I'd been making this journey every night for the last week.

The air tickled the back of my damp neck and I turned around, even though no one was there. I heard a long shriek, an owl scream. It flew low over my head and I ducked, even though it wasn't low enough to hit me. I stopped when I saw the door. It was open, creaking back and forth by itself like a gift. This would be easier than climbing up the wall to the window ledge.

I crept into the kitchen. I'd never been this far in before. It was empty, all the noise coming from the main taproom; shouting, screaming, singing and laughing, all fuelled by the drinks Henry poured.

Emilia sat still in the rocking chair. She'd long since stopped cooking, there was only a small fire with a black kettle hanging on a hook. The room was full of empty plates: a devoured carcass of a chicken sat on the table along with other meats, all covered in flies, which buzzed and hummed as I moved around the room. She hadn't been able to clear the plates away, they'd just been dumped on the table next to her. The room was a mess, food and drinks and dirt everywhere, and Emilia sat in the middle of it, immobile and for once silent, not talking, talking, talking at me.

I stopped to look at her as moonlight slunk into the room. The light softened her, making her look like a woman rather than a witch.

I moved to the windowsill, taking care to avoid the knives that stuck out at odd angles near the table edge. I inched my way to the bowl. I knew she'd have taken the ring off to wash the plates. I knew she would have drunk too much to remember to put it back on. I knew this because I'd been watching her for days, waiting out in the dark for almost a week, monitoring her every move, noting her routine. Until I knew what I needed to do.

On the windowsill was a bowl. The purse was nowhere to be seen, but glinting and shining in the moonlight was the ring. *My ring.* I put it on my own finger, where it sat, snug and safe. I took the stone ring out of my pocket and placed it in the bowl and next to it I put the fresh vial of medicine I'd made earlier. I removed the old one, tucking it away in my pocket, hiding the evidence. It was almost empty. They were the same shape and I'd known she would never think to check. I turned back to look at her and saw a large tankard next to her on the table. I leant over and picked it up. It was empty, she'd drunk it all.

I heard someone running past the window and ducked down by her feet, almost dropping the tankard. I crouched low and clutched it in my hand, like a weapon, hoping that they weren't coming in, that Henry hadn't sent one of his friends to come and check on Emilia. Their feet clomped past the open stable door and didn't slow or stop. I raised myself up. I could hear them shouting and laughing, their voices echoing down the path. I replaced the tankard next to her and breathed out in relief.

Henry brings Emilia a tankard of beer every night, after she's finished cooking. She puts it on the windowsill next to her ring. She tips some of the vial into the tankard, swirls it around and drinks it down. She then has a smoke and a chat through the stable door with whoever is passing, finishes the last of the ale and goes back into the kitchen to wash the plates. Once she's finished, she puts her ring back on, ready to join Henry in the taproom and dazzle everyone with her gold and emeralds and more drink. It is the same every night, always in that order.

Every night, except tonight.

He must have been in to see her and presumed her drunk or asleep and left her to it. I hoped she was just asleep, but I wasn't sure so I placed my hand under her nose. I'd been careful with the levels in the vial, but it wasn't an exact science. I felt her slow, low breath tickle the hairs on the back of my hand. She was fine. Tomorrow she would wake and see the stone ring in the bowl and the fresh vial on the windowsill, but by then it would be too late. I would have left and all she'd have to remember me by would be her anger and an aching head.

I took the drawing out of my pocket and unfolded it so that when she finally woke up she'd see it. She'd take in what she'd been asking to see for so long: her future. The drawing would show her what happens to people like her, bad people who do bad things. I needed her to see what I had. See herself be led down a narrow damp corridor with chains and metal circles around her wrists, justice holding her captive. I wanted to watch her being taken away from her family, from her friends, if she has any. I drew her trapped, imprisoned, unable to defend herself with her quick words and wicked lies. I wondered how long it would take for her to realise what the drawing was showing her. I'd done as I was told, at last. I'd been a good boy and drawn her future, hers and Henry's.

I wanted to kick her, to hit her in her face, push her to the floor and smash her head into the ground.

But I didn't.

I set the drawing down on the table, placing the tankard on top so it wouldn't blow away, and left her with it. I shut the stable door behind me. I had one place left to go, one person to say goodbye to before I collected Dog and our things and left, forever.

CHAPTER 23
NOAH

I am drawing the river again. I've been dreaming about it too – I'm running through the water as if I am trying to get away from it, but my legs don't work. I can't run or jump over whatever force is stopping me. I try to climb the rapids, foamy white steps which lead to nowhere. I keep drawing it, over and over, even though it makes no sense. At the edge of the picture is a dog running fast. His legs and tail are all that's left in the frame. He looks like he's trying to escape from the page, like he's running from something in the river.

'Did someone teach you to draw like that?' Beth asks, watching the shapes form on the page, trying her best to understand me. We are sitting under the shade of the silver birches that run along the top of the school field like a prison wall, keeping us in and the rest of the village out.

'I don't know, I don't think so. I've always drawn like this, before I started school even. Sometimes I try and stop drawing and think about other things, but then I look down and I am doing it anyway. So I give up.' I lift my hands up and then let them fall, as if that's all it was, just drawing and nothing more. Something I could just throw away if I wanted to.

'Why don't you do something else then?' she suggests, as if drawing is a pastime to me, something I have power over.

'That's why I go running. I try to tire myself out, to run and run so that when I go to bed I just crash out,' I answer. She carries on regardless.

'How about getting your dad to teach you photography? Hey, I know! You could learn to play an instrument. *I could teach how to play the piano*! I think you'd be really good at it, you're a fast learner. My piano teacher thinks I'll make an ace music teacher. I'd love to do that. You could just fill all your spare time with loads of different stuff, so that there's no time to draw!' Her brown eyes open wide as the idea hits her.

'It's a nice idea, but it's not something I can start or stop. I don't have any choice in it, Beth. If I did then don't you think I'd have stopped ages ago? I just *have* to draw. Even if I fill every second of the day with something, I draw in my sleep.' I sound like an addict and I can see she's thinking something similar. I can hear how melodramatic my words are.

'My mum does this really good hypno thing, you know, hypnotherapy. She does hypno-birthing CDs to stop women feeling the pain, apparently it works. No, *wait, wait!*' She starts giggling when she sees the face I'm pulling. 'I'm not saying that CD for you, *obviously*! She's got loads of CDs of her voice talking and music and stuff. She gives them to her patients, well, patients who need a bit of help with sleeping properly and other stuff.'

I must have stopped laughing because she stares at me.

'It isn't like being hypnotised, not like those stupid TV shows you see where someone's made to act like a chicken, Noah. This is really different; it's a bit like a relaxation exercise but better. I've used it. I've got the one for sleep problems. It definitely works; you can borrow it. I used to have this one dream about a witch dragging her bony fingers down my windowsill and then she'd press her bluey grey palm up against my window and wave at me. Turns out it was one of the trees scraping down the windowpane, anyway, this CD helped me go to sleep, after I made Dad cut the tree down!' She drags her fingers down an imaginary window and does a fake cackle.

'I can't see a CD helping me, Beth. It's not a case of putting my mind to something. I don't have any control over this part of my mind. It's like I'm on autopilot. Something else takes over and I can't stop it. I've tried.' I know she means well but I want her to stop trying to help. She reminds me of my dad always trying to fix things, just making me feel more broken.

'But Mum does serious ones too, for smokers and other stuff, like OCD. You should ask her to make you one, *not that I'm saying you've got OCD or anything*. You know what

I mean, don't you? You know for people who can't stop.' She looks awkward, as if she might have overstepped the mark and hurt me with words like OCD. I wish I had OCD or even that I smoked and needed to give up like Theo. These sound like simple things to sort out, in comparison anyway. If I thought a CD would send me to sleep and fix it all, I'd go and get one today, but I knew there was no way. *No way.*

I unclench my fists and breathe in and out quietly. I need to explain it better, but it isn't an easy thing to talk about. I feel like a fraud because I'm not giving her the full story. If I told her everything, told her what I did that day, then she'd know that there's no magic wand to wave here. Some things can't be fixed and I'm one of them.

'It's like I'm underwater. It takes over my brain. Sometimes I forget to breathe out properly and I'll do a massive sigh and nearly choke. It's like resurfacing after you've done a dive. You don't quite know if you'll make it back up to the top in time. But when you do the relief is huge.'

She's really trying, leaning forwards into me, listening to everything, playing with her necklace. She'd put the other stone on there too, the one I'd found in her garden. Beth opens her mouth to offer another solution, but I can't bear to hear her eager voice full of hope and happiness and answers.

'Look, Beth, I've tried to stop drawing before, but I can't,

OK? I've tried really hard. It might sound strange to have a talent or gift and then want to fight it, but I do. I feel like I'm the only one in the whole world. Like I'm marooned by these images flying all around me, but I can't catch them quickly enough to make sense of it all…' I can't tell her what I mean. I don't have the right words.

I stop drawing and close my art book, trying to shut away the storm that's building, but she's still watching me, ready to keep going until she comes up with an idea that'll work. And I don't have the heart to tell her to stop.

I get up and start walking quickly down the field, pulling her along with me. She has to run to keep up. I need to get back into school and a busy hallway full of people calling 'Shut up!', 'Tuck that shirt in!' and 'Walk, don't run please!' I want to be pushed and shoved in the corridor as I try to get my stuff out of my locker for the next lesson. I need to not think. Not to hear everything in my head going round and round like a washing machine on an endless spin cycle.

CHAPTER 24
BLAZE

I didn't know which unmarked grave was hers, so I visited all the paupers' graves. I placed damp ox-eye daisies on all of the nameless mounds and said a prayer for all of them, all the lost souls from the workhouse and worse places. They rest on the other side of the graveyard wall, not allowed in the holy ground where those with money lie in perfect peace. The boundary wall divides the two and I knew on which side of it I stood. I knelt down on the soil and wet grass and said goodbye to Maman. I took off the emerald ring and hung it on my necklace next to her sacred stones, *pierres sacrées*. I knew they would keep me safe.

I tucked the necklace out of sight, crossed myself and asked for her blessing before I left. I knew she would want me to find my way back to her home. I left the church grounds and chose to walk down the long path past the Manor House for the last time. I stopped by the long pond and watched the rainbow fish darting about, quicksilver comets of light and colour. I walked on, touching the tall herbs in my mother's kitchen garden with the tips of my fingers one last time, releasing the scents and smells that reminded me of her into the air. I stood in the moonlight and looked up at the old Manor House, the place where we were once happy, and felt that this was the right decision. To leave.

I wanted to see the world, to see *her* world, a place I've only ever visited in stories. It's time.

Everything changed tonight for Dog and me.

I walked under the arbour away from the Manor House towards my hidden hut. But the stillness didn't last.

My door was broken, hanging by a hinge in the breeze. One of the panels was smashed in and the window was cracked. Something was lying across the threshold and the door creaked back and forth, banging into it, unable to shut. I knew I shut it when I left. I always did because if I didn't the heat made it bigger and then it would never shut again. I looked about for Dog, clicking my tongue, but I couldn't see him in the dark. My hand went into my coat pocket and wrapped around my knife. I tested my finger against the blade. I took care to keep it sharp.

I looked all around me. There was no one in the dark garden.

I was on my own.

But my stomach told me something smelt wrong. The stench got stronger as I took each slow step to my hut. I put my hand over my mouth, gagging. The smell of sick was in the air, but there was a sharpness to it, a smell I didn't recognise. I breathed in deeply, through my mouth rather than my nose, and forced myself forwards. Whatever was behind the door was waiting for me, but before I could open it, I tripped over something solid. I shouted out a sound, a frightened noise, and held my hands up ready for an attack, but no one moved. I looked down at my feet and my eyes made out a shape.

A body lying motionless.

I dropped to my knees. Dog was lying across the doorway and he smelt wrong, unnatural, and was breathing every other breath. His tail didn't move as he saw me, as he smelt me. It didn't thump up and down. I put my hands on his stomach and he groaned weakly. I whispered, telling him I would help him. Around his muzzle dripped a green foam and the wrong smell came from inside his mouth. I heaved as I put my nose to his, to try and guess the smell. It was garlic but that didn't make sense. Garlic wouldn't make Dog ill. He must have eaten or drunk something else, something poisonous. I had to get it out. I hooked my finger gently into his soft mouth to clear it and he growled low at me. I patted him gently over and over on his shoulder, to show him I was going to help him, I would make him better. I told him *I would never hurt you.* He lifted his head awkwardly and in the moonlight I could see his eyes. They were tired and his face was crumpled. It was a struggle for him to keep them open.

I looked past him into my hut, ready to get the

medicine that would make him better, but everything was on the floor. My small table was upside down and my stool was broken into sharp splinters. The rush mat I slept on had been burnt to ashes. All my herbs, vials, pots and small bowls were smashed. The floor was covered in basil, ginger, chamomile and fennel and I could smell something else, something sour: piss.

There was nothing left for Dog. It was all gone, stamped into the floor, ruined and wasted. What could I give him now? How would I save him? I started to get up, to try and find something to heal him, anything, but he put his heavy rough paw on my knee and I didn't move an inch.

His big cracked paw was hot and damp. The black nails were long and scratched at my skin as his legs twitched and shook violently. I touched his nose, which was dry when it should have been damp. I held his big black head in both my hands, like the heaviest weight, and looked into his eyes as he whimpered and whined softly. I told him *I love you*. I told him to *hold on, just wait*.

But he couldn't. His dark eyes closed and I knew they wouldn't open again. His last breath went in but didn't come back out.

CHAPTER 25
NOAH

When we get back to Beth's, we watch *Edward Scissorhands* again, quoting lines to each other as they said them on the screen. I hold Beth's copy of *The Corpse Bride* in one hand and my copy of *Beetlejuice* in the other, but Beth shakes her head chanting, '*Homework, homework, homework,*' at me and as we're in her house I can't really argue.

'Were you even listening to Mr Bourne in History?' Beth asks. I shrug at her. 'Did you hand your form in for the History trip?' she continues and I shake my head.

'Where are we going?' I ask. I'd drifted in and out a bit in Mr Bourne's last lesson.

'Noah! He's been talking about it for weeks. We're going to the workhouse in Halstead. You have to get your mum to sign it or you'll have to stay at school and there's no way I'm going on my own. Not with Eva the way she is at the moment.' Beth looks uncomfortable.

'OK. I'll get Mum to sign it tonight. I swear, I'll remember,' I promise her. I wouldn't let her go on her own and a trip would make a nice change, even if it was educational.

'So I take it you weren't listening to anything Mr Bourne said, then?' Beth asks.

I hold my hands up in surrender as she fills me in. Turns out the most well-known tragedy to take place in Sible Hedingham began with The Swan Inn swimmings. As part of our History module with Mr Bourne, we were learning about our village's past and following our family trees. We'd found out that several members of the class, not me obviously, but Beth and a few others, could trace their ancestors back to Halstead Workhouse, Hedingham Castle, Melford Hall and other key historical sites.

'It was the last swimming of an accused witch in the whole country, and it made Sible Hedingham famous! Witches had stopped being swum or ducked ages ago, so the Sible Hedingham Witchcraft case was even more shocking,' she continues. As she reads, I look at the diagrams I've sketched on the corner of my worksheet.

'The women's right thumb would be tied to their left toe and their left thumb to their right toe. Then they were thrown into the water. If they sank they were declared innocent, whether they drowned or not, but if they floated then they were definitely a witch and met death at the stake.' She pauses to take another bite from her cookie.

The stupidity and cruelty makes me feel explosive. I want to stand on her kitchen table and shout, *'This is off the charts mad!'* But of course it all happened a long time ago, so I keep my temper, stay in my chair and gesture at her to carry on reading. I like listening to her voice.

'On the 3rd of August 1865 a French boy, Blaze Ambroise, who had a reputation as a fortune teller, was accused of putting a curse on a woman called Emilia Rawlinson. Emilia Rawlinson is said to have accused the "foreigner Ambroise" of cursing her with Lyme's disease.'

'That's just unreal. *A curse?*' I want her to stop but she doesn't notice and carries on.

'It says here that the victim only communicated by a few words and his drawings, as English was not his first language. He lived somewhere in the village, having run away from the workhouse. The gipsy was always accompanied by his dog and wore several hats all at the same time. He was consulted by the local girls as a recognised authority on courtship and marriage. He also made herbal potions for villagers to heal ailments and common complaints.' She finally finishes.

'So just because he looked a bit weird and dressed funny and pretended to tell fortunes, he was accused of being able to curse someone, of being a *witch*?' I ask. I don't really know why I'm pretending not to understand. I know well enough what people are like about this kind of thing: about telling fortunes, trying to see into the future, mediums, clairvoyants, mystics, fortune-tellers and anyone who is a bit different.

'It says here that "Even 130 years ago in rural Essex the fear of witchcraft was a firmly held belief in the minds of country people,"' Beth reads.

'But that's ages ago. 1865? Things have changed a lot since then,' I argue.

She looks at me long and hard and then reaches into her school bag.

'I was going to give you this earlier, but there were too many people about at school.' Her head down, she rummages in her bag. She pulls out a small velvet drawstring bag. It looks like it came from a gift shop and I wonder what is in it. She drops it into my hand.

'It's not my birthday or anything.' I feel awkward. I don't have anything for her.

'I know. *I know* when your birthday is, it's not for that! I just wanted to give you something this time. It's not a handwritten quote or a bunch of weeds...'

'*Hey*! They were wild flowers, beautiful wild flowers picked with care!' I throw a handful of raisins at her that she'd picked out of her cookie earlier.

'OK, OK! *Flowers*. Anyway, I wanted you to know that, even though we haven't talked about it properly that much ... well, I believe you, about what you told me, in your room. I trust you and I wanted to give you something to show you that, I guess.' She stops and waits for me to open the bag.

I pull it open and take out a long thin black cord. A single stone hangs from it, a pale stone with a hole in, the one I found in her garden. I look back at her neck, she is wearing the other stone, the one she found. They are almost identical.

148

'I can't take one of your stones.' I shake my head. It is too much.

'Yes, you can. I want you to. It'll keep you safe. I know it sounds silly but I really believe it. It's not a charm or anything, but it's special. Did I ever tell you where I found my stone?'

She picks it up out of my hand and stands up behind me. She starts talking again as she holds it around my neck, ready to tie it. I can feel the goosebumps on the back of my neck as her hot hands hover next to my skin.

'When we first moved in, no one had lived in the Manor for years. I remember finding the hut under a mass of ivy in the snow. It felt like my own secret garden. When I was clearing the ivy off to get to the door, I found something, a stone under the snow, and as I searched I found more, all around the summer house like a trail, going round and round in a circle. There were small pretty stones, big lumps of quartz and a few tiny shells. And inside the hut I found this stone, it felt so different to all the others, light and soft. When I held the stone it was sun warm as if it was a scorching hot day, *like today*. But we moved into the house in the winter.' She holds the two ends of the necklace as she talks; still not ready to tie the knot.

'The funniest thing about these hot stones is the holes in them. I've never seen stones like it. The holes are so perfect and round, they look like they've been made from a machine, but I just know they haven't. When I found it

I hid it in my jewellery box. After a while I threaded it onto an old necklace and started wearing it. This might sound strange but the stone makes me feel safe, safe and warm. And then you found this one and now it will do the same for you, I hope,' she says as she finally ties it but keeps her hands on my shoulders.

I can feel her breath on the hairs at the back of my neck. For a second I think she might lean in and kiss me. She is so close, I can hear her breathe softly in her throat. She puts her hands on either side of my neck and presses her lips really slowly against my skin, warm and gentle. I turn around to face her as she sits down on my lap. I kiss her back as her parents come noisily through the front door, shouting about Beth's brilliant comments at parents' evening. Beth climbs off my lap and moves away as they walk into the room, filling it with their laughter, praise for their daughter and the smell of fish and chips.

When I get home Mum is rushing out the door to parents' evening, having had to take a later appointment because of Dad.

'Ah, at last, you're home. Right, here's a list to keep you busy while we're out. Dad's meeting me there. There's a pizza in the oven. Hope I'm going to hear good things about you!' She kisses me, wipes the trace of lipstick off my cheek and grabs her keys. 'Don't forget to put the wheelie bins out, will you? The recycling one's nearly overflowing,' she shouts over her shoulder before shutting the front door.

The list she's written is endless. The first item is to weed and water the kitchen garden. She likes to call it a *kitchen garden* but it was really just a vegetable patch. We had a much bigger one in the last place. I wonder if she resented leaving it behind? If she resented me? There isn't much to weed, Mum is on top of things like that, so I connect up the hose and turn the water on. The second item on the list is to put the wheelie bins in the collection area. There is a communal one at the end of our road.

The sun starts to slip down the sky as I drag the green recycling bin down the drive, round the corner and dump it in the fenced-off area. As I slam the back gate shut, I hear shouting from over the fence. I turn the water down to low sprinkle and look up. There is a kid sitting in the frame of the window. It's the kid in the drawing, Eva's brother. His back is to the open window and I can hear him arguing with someone, or trying to. It sounds like he is losing the fight. He keeps leaning further back, the small seat of his jeans hanging very slightly over the window ledge.

I don't know whether to call up to the kid and risk scaring him, or to run over to the house and tell our neighbour what's going on upstairs. If it had been anyone's house but Eva's, I would have done. I would have told his mum that her son was hanging out the window, that he wasn't safe. But I didn't. *I couldn't.*

I stand there, panic charging into all my nerve endings, setting my teeth on edge. Spit is pooling in my mouth and I know the longer I wait the more dangerous the situation will get. I know this and I can't stand by and do nothing, not again. I feel like shouting, 'Help, help me!' but this could make the kid jump and fall.

And then I see her, standing in front of him. I can picture the smile on her face. I know it off by heart.

She is shouting and sniping at him. Then she undoes her tie, pulling the knot loose and unthreading it. I know where this is going, but I don't know how it will end. I haven't drawn that. I hear his weaker voice battle back and then she fills the window, leaning over him as her hands go to his throat. She wraps her school tie around his neck then tilts him back and forth like a seesaw, as his arms spin around, trying to push her away.

His head is completely out of the window now, hovering in the air, his arms flapping and he's screaming, pleading with her. But she doesn't stop. I can't make out the words but I can hear the tone in his voice, desperate.

I shout out 'STOP!' as loudly as I can and run to the fence. I try to get up and over, but my baseball boots are useless, I just slide back down. I bang the fence with my fists and shout out again, stupid things like 'No!' or 'Wait! Stop! Someone help me?' as loud as possible, as if Eva would even hear me, but the shouting and the crying stop. I kick my boots off and manage to get up on top of the fence in my socks.

The kid is panicking, trying to push her back, wobbling them both dangerously. His hands are in the air, reaching for her, as he tries to pull at her tie. He is going to pull her out of the window with him if I don't do something!

'EVA! *Noooooooooooooo!*' I scream, as long and as loud as I can.

She grabs the kid around the waist, hauling him back into the bedroom and ducks out of sight. Her brother is sobbing and I can hear Eva saying, 'Sorry, sorry, I'm sorry alright?' over and over.

She sticks her head out of the window and looks around, but doesn't see me. Her eyes are searching for something and then I see what: her tie on the patio beneath the window. She must have heard someone shouting and stopped. She must have heard me.

I slide back down the fence and stand in my socks in the mud, feeling shaky and tired but so relieved. I laugh, watching the water run all over the vegetable patch flooding the bed, but I couldn't care less.

I stopped her. I'd seen what she was going to do, I'd drawn it and then I'd stopped it from happening. I hadn't drawn the ending because I'd determined it. I'd made the ending happen.

For the first time in my life my drawing means

something. It's useful and not sad or threatening like …
like all the others. Like that first time.

This time *I* stopped it.

CHAPTER 26
BLAZE

They took me quickly and carefully, as if they'd rehearsed it. They must have already worked out who would do what, because I was off the floor and in the air before I knew what was happening.

I hadn't moved for hours, not since Dog left me. I'd been lying on the ground, wrapped around his slowly chilling body, but now I was wide awake.

One man had my feet and the other my arms. I was thrown up and over his great shoulder. I could smell him, Henry: he stank of ale and smoke. I shouted and kicked, digging my fists into his back, but he held me so tight and firm I couldn't get down, no matter how hard I struggled. All the blood rushed to my head as he climbed over the fence, with me still slung over his shoulder. He ran down the river path as if I weighed nothing at all. My head banged against the back of his legs over and over as panic set in.

I could hear someone running next to him, muttering something to him. The sounds of the river crashed in my ears. I could hear the rapids and the roar as he ran along the river path, on and on. I dropped my hands and stopped kicking. His pace slowed until he stopped running and walked quickly instead, sensing I'd given up the fight. I kept up the pretence as best I could, biding my time, searching for the right moment.

He threw me to the ground and pointed at me, holding a lantern up to my face. There was a crowd, a group of men who must have followed Henry from The Swan. A cluster of women with scarves around their heads were coming over the bridge from the village, all staring at me. Henry started to speak, shouting, trying to raise the crowd's anger to match his own.

'See this boy? You've seen him, haven't you? Yes, we all have. Skulking about the village like a thief in the night, well, we've had enough of it. He took Emilia's ring. He came into the kitchen tonight and took my Emilia's ring, creeping in like a river rat while she slept. And you can bet he's taken something from all of you, oh yes, you can be sure of that. I know what's been going on, she's told me, she's been watching you all, see, and she's been watching him. You're all guilty, each one of you, and it's time to put a stop to it.'

He pointed at the women in the crowd who had reluctantly come over the bridge and down to the riverside, their talking and laughing replaced by a tense silence. This crowd parted to reveal Emilia and her wide smile. Clearly I'd got the measurements wrong and hadn't given her anywhere near enough. She looked dazed, but anger boiled up in her eyes as she approached me.

'See Emilia's hands? See what he's done to her?'

Someone gasped in the crowd and I heard a, *'No, no,'* as Henry held Emilia's hands up for all to see. They were swollen, red and lumpy, just as they had been before I'd started treating her. One night off her medicine and she'd got her claws back. Her raw skin had risen and was scorched like a burn and of course her ring finger was empty and naked.

'Yes! Yes he did! He's been selling her medicine, telling her he'll make her better, but look here is the evidence for you all to see. He's been poisoning her, making her worse! And none of you are safe, none of you women are safe with this gipsy in the village. Who knows what potions and poisons he's been making your wives, sisters, mothers and daughters?'

He changed tack and started talking to the men, pointing at them and I saw their faces change right in front of me. They looked uncertain and scared, shifting, moving into one another to form a crowd, a mob.

'And there's more, isn't there? We all know the worst of it, we've all been turning our backs to what's been going on in this village, but now he's shown his true colours. He's been casting spells like a sorcerer.' He paused to let that sink in. It took some of the men by surprise.

'He's been looking into times he shouldn't, claiming to tell us what will happen, what will become of us. Telling us tall tales about our futures!'

He held up my drawing and shook it at me, proof of my sorcery, evidence of my witchcraft. No one was close enough to see Emilia in shackles or Henry in handcuffs. But it was enough, just the suggestion on paper, the suspicion of the future. The lines from my pencils and charcoal have sealed my fate.

'You've been playing a dangerous game here, boy, but your time is up now. No one here wants to play these games with you no more.' He looked around at his crowd, who were shaking their heads in agreement, calling out, 'That's right', 'I won't be taken for a fool', 'Tell him, Henry, you tell him', followed by a hiss of, '*Witch*'.

I can almost feel the crowd turn.

Witch

I caution myself to wait.

Witch

To watch.

Witch

And not to panic.

'Yes! He's a *witch*, that's what he is. He's a witch and we know what to do with 'im, don't we? We know what happens to witches, to devil worshippers like 'im.' He crowed the last bit out, raising his head and his voice. The crowd couldn't stand still now, desperate to act, to join in, itching to do *something*.

The grass was wet underneath my back. I tried to inch away from him as he addressed the crowd, but Emilia gave me a sharp kick to my ribs rolling me backwards. All the eyes of the village were on me, narrowing, getting darker, angrier as Henry poisoned their minds against me.

'So we'll test 'im. We'll see if his powers can save 'im, if his magic and spells and potions and pictures can tell 'im how to get out of this.' He held up a line of rope like a showman entertaining a crowd. He tied it tightly around my wrists. I fought him, losing my hat to the river, as I was dragged over to the edge. I dug my heels in the ground, but my boots had fallen off and the soles of my feet slipped uselessly in the mud.

Henry held me by the back of my shirt, tipping me over, leaning my body out in the air above the water.

'*Witches* aren't welcome here. Foreigners who lie and cheat and steal aren't welcome here. Curses and black magic aren't welcome in our village. So, as many have said before me standing over this very pool, I say: begone, witch, *begone*! I cast you out, witch.' His throat rasped from all the shouting, and then I heard nothing as he plunged me into the water, feet first, his big hands holding my head under.

Now I fought back.

Now I wriggled and kicked and pushed my feet down against the riverbed with all the force I could gather. I held my last breath tight in my lungs, straining against the pressure, as I thrashed up to the surface and came face to face with Henry.

He looked surprised, his eyes wildly flicking from me to the crowd. He leaned forwards to push me under again and then he stopped. Something had caught his eye.

'What's this?' he hissed at me, forgetting the role he was playing, forgetting the crowd. He pulled me out of the water, reaching past my shirt, his thick hands at my neck, and hooked out my necklace. Hanging from it were my mother's stones and the ring, which he couldn't take his eyes off.

'What's this then?' he asked, shouting it out loud now, ready to make the most of this moment. 'My Emilia's ring, hanging around the thief's neck. Proof, I tell you! Evidence of his crime in my hands!'

He grabbed the necklace and tore it from my neck, ripping my skin. The cord snapped and, for a second, paused in the air between his hand and my body, and then the stones and the ring flew off the cord, arched high in the air and landed with a soft splash in the river.

This was the moment I'd been waiting for.

The stones had saved me.

His hold loosened and I broke away.

And ran.

I ran past Henry, who was staring like a madman into the water. I saw Emilia throw herself into the water as I reached the top of the bridge. I heard the screams of the women and the shouting men, trying to pull her out. I heard Henry and others pursue me as I jumped down from the bridge onto the path. I ran past The Swan, ignoring their shouts and threats. I ran on and on up the high street.

Someone caught hold of the back of my shirt and lifted me off the ground, pulling me through a doorway and shutting it firmly behind me.

I fell onto the floor, heaving, desperate for air.

'Shut up. Just shut up, boy. Get behind that door. Now.' A man shoved me into a cupboard barely big enough to hold me. It was dark and smelt of wood.

'Stay in there, I'll tell you when it's clear.' The voice was familiar but I couldn't place it. I couldn't breathe properly, let alone speak. My neck was sore and my throat dry and cracked. I did as I was told. I didn't have much choice.

'They've gone. It's clear. Open the door, Aileen,' he said some time later.

'I canny guess what they were thinking of. *Wha kind o'madness is this*?' A woman's voice this time and one I recognised. It was the farrier's wife. She opened the cupboard door. I could smell wood smoke and tea as she helped me out.

'Hush now, pet, hush now, y'safe now. Thomas's got ye, we'll see you safe,' she soothed, her voice carrying me away from the river, the crowd and the whispering water as I collapsed onto her cold kitchen floor.

CHAPTER 27
NOAH

Mum's been really weird all evening. I try to work out what I've done but give up. I'm getting the silent treatment, which is ten times worse than being shouted at – at least that gets it over with. Maybe I've left my running kit on the floor in the utility room again? I can't see why that would stress her out so much. When Dad gets in, they go off upstairs together. I can hear them arguing, but can't make out the words. After a few minutes a door opens upstairs and their voices filter down into the kitchen.

'Take a look, Daniel. Tell me if this is normal? They said that he'd been doodling in his exercise books, inside his History textbook, for goodness sake. It's starting again, isn't it? Another nightmare, that's what this is, another *bloody nightmare!*' Mum shouts at Dad.

It's quiet for a minute or two, then I hear my dad swear.

I try to get out of the kitchen before they come down, but I'm too slow. I have nowhere to go. I can't walk out. If I did, I'd still have to come home eventually and whatever this is would still be here, waiting for me. I hear one of them coming along the hallway. I feel sick, knowing this is about more than a few detentions or muddy trainers.

Luckily, it's my dad and not my mum. I can hear her crying upstairs, which is even worse than her coming down and shouting at me. I've made her cry! Shit.

Dad sits at the kitchen table and puts down my History textbook. He opens it to a page covered in scribbles and black lines, then another page with colours – blues, midnights, blacks, navys, dark greens, watery colours – all running over the pages like fingerprints.

'There were some comments at parents' evening about your constant drawing, or "doodling" they called it. Apparently you've drawn over some of your textbooks and worksheets. The teacher found them. So your mum went through your school bag and found this. I wish she hadn't, to be honest.'

He shows it to me. It's a page full of colour and rips and tears. In the middle of the drawing is a bone, discoloured and decayed, set on a step like an offering or a sacrifice.

'Want to tell me what this is?' he asks, as if he doesn't have the energy for long sentences, he's talked enough upstairs.

I shake my head, feeling stupid.

He stands up and starts ripping the page up, tearing sheets out of my maths book. Some fall onto the floor as he spits at me, 'You promised me! You promised us you'd never, ever draw this kind of thing again. Who on earth do you think you are? What are we going to do with you?'

He looks at me as if *I* can make any more sense of this than him. He shakes his head, turns his back and strides across the kitchen, then he changes his mind and swings back, charging over to me. Bits of paper fly up into the air like confetti as he stands over me.

'I don't understand you, I really don't. Why would you draw such, such *horrible things*? For God's sake! A bone? Someone's actual bone? Why would you draw that? All that water too. It looks like someone's drowned. It looks like someone is there under the water. Is that what this is? Is someone going to die?' He looks desperate, his eyes wide in horror, as he searches through the images, clutching at them.

'I don't know, Dad. That's the problem. I just don't know. It doesn't make any sense to me.' I feel panicked and useless. I've scared him, I can see it in his face. I am freaking him out. I'm freaking myself out.

'Then just stop it. It's rubbish, total nonsense. If you don't know what or who it's about, then stop drawing it, for God's sake!' Dad shouts at me, raising his hands as if he could command me, the paper clenched in his fists. 'You've really upset your mother. Again. Just when she thought you were settling down, making friends, being normal, you start drawing someone's body and bones in the water. I mean, where is this, Noah? Is this in a river? I feel like I should do something, but I've got nothing to go on! Is this even real? I'm talking to you as if this is real, as if you can know! I'm going mad here.' He slaps his hand against his forehead, as if the whole thing's crazy. He's right; it does sound impossible. But we both know it isn't. He just doesn't want to face it. But I have to.

He searches the pictures for the answers. Then he lets them go. For a moment my drawings are floating above us, until they fall down, spilling onto the floor. I see long tendrils of wet black hair curling around a face, eyes shut and mouth open in silent horror, like a mermaid. Her hands reach up and outwards trying to claw their way back up to the surface.

'I don't know, Dad. I keep telling you, but it's not the same as before. This is different, I promise.' I try to reason with him, turning away from the pictures on the floor.

I have to keep drawing. I have to see what's going to happen. This time it could be something I can stop. I can't hide from this.

'I can stop it this time,' I whisper, the words creeping out of me just loud enough for him to hear.

'If you're talking about what I think you're talking about, I don't want to hear it, Noah. We said we wouldn't talk about that again.' He stands up. 'I can't do this.' He towers over me, his lips closed as if he can just zip them up and never let the words out. Well, I won't do that any more. I can't keep quiet, letting things fester. I jump up to try to meet his height, wondering if we'll be level one day – equal.

'You can't talk about what happened and call it *'that'*. She *died*, Dad! Grace died and I could have stopped it. I should have stopped it, but I didn't know how. I didn't get what the drawing was showing me. *How could I?* I'd only just turned five. It wasn't MY fault!' I shout at him and he looks shocked, staggering back from me.

'No one ever said it was your fault, Noah. Of course it wasn't your fault. It was an awful tragedy. No one ever blamed you. We never blamed you. But you promised us. You said you could make it stop.'

'But I can't, that's the problem. I keep promising you both, and I mean it at the time, but I can't help it!'

I look at him. 'I drew her in the garden, in the paddling pool with her hair floating up to the surface. I drew it before it happened, Dad. Then I hid it in my toy box. I should have shown someone. *I should have told someone.* I should have told you or Mum. But I knew it was wrong. I can see myself right now shoving it to the bottom of the box, wishing it would fly away or disappear.' It feels so good finally to say the words, say what I'd seen and done.

But he's saying, *'No, no, no,'* under his breath, like a mantra getting louder and louder as he paces around the kitchen, trampling the pictures into the floor tiles.

'No! *No!* You need to see another doctor. We can't just hope for the best, or that you'll grow out of it or learn to control it. There must be a way to stop you from drawing in this way. I mean, you can't go through the rest of your life drawing things that happen to people, not knowing where or when, can you? It's just not right, Noah. It's no life for you, or for us.'

He sits down again next to me and puts his hands softly on my shoulders, forcing me to look at him.

'Noah, you've got to take control now. I believe in you and your mum believes in you and what you say about your drawing, but that doesn't mean you can carry on like this. This isn't right, mate. Your mother can't take any more of this and neither can I. We'll get you some help, whatever it takes. We love you, Noah, are you listening to me? We love you, son.'

He looks at me, desperate for me to give him what he wants. He carries on talking, getting louder and more agitated.

'I think we both thought things had changed this time, after the move. You seemed to be settling down so well but clearly we were wrong. Clearly *NOTHING HAS CHANGED!*' He shouts the last bit and then goes silent.

He gets up and flings any remaining bits of paper off the table onto the kitchen floor with the rest. I don't know what to say. He's shaking, red in the face just looking at me, and I'm properly scared because I've never seen him like this. *Raging.* I lean back a bit, to move away, but he grips my chair and tilts it so that he's right in my face, so close I can feel his breath on my cheek. He holds my chair there, balancing on two legs, and then lets it fall back down with a crash, moving away from me, as if he doesn't quite trust himself. We're both out of breath and lost.

Eventually he bends down and picks up every single piece of paper off the floor, whispering something over and over. I lower my head to hear.

'*Grace, Grace, Grace.*'

I turn away, but I find myself whispering too.

'I'm sorry.'

When I look back, the kitchen door is wide open. He switches off the light in the hallway, climbs the stairs slowly and then shuts their bedroom door. I am on my own, again.

I sit there in the dark silence, trying to promise myself not to draw those pictures again, knowing that I will. Knowing that I'll draw them over and over and over in more and more detail, etching out the lines and veins and skin on that bone. And each picture will be worse than the one before and there's nothing my dad, my mum or a doctor can do to stop it.

I know that I'll draw until I see the ink move, twitching and twisting under my eyelids like flesh and bone, clawing away at me until something comes into focus, something that makes sense. I have to wait for the images to become clear and develop into a picture.

CHAPTER 28
BLAZE

'D'you think he can hear us, Thomas? *Can you hear me, pet?* Put him down there, in the wee cot.' I felt someone put me down on a bed. Footsteps tapped around the room. My stinging skin was being rubbed with cloth, up and down my arms, until I could feel them properly again. I opened my eyes. A little girl with long white hair was staring at me, her thumb in her mouth.

'Hush away now, Caitlin, move. Give him this, Thomas, it'll help.' He passed me a cup with what smelt like hot sweet tea. I was inside, it was warm, but I could hear my teeth clacking against each other. The child hovered between the man and the woman. It was the farrier, his wife, and their child.

'What happened? Can y'tell us what happened, pet?' the woman asked. I shook my head. I didn't know where to start.

'We need to move him, Aileen. We can't keep him here, it's too dangerous.' The farrier spoke to his wife in a low whisper, but both the child and I could hear them. She was smiling at me, singing something gently to me in a language I couldn't understand, as the farrier left the cottage. The room was starting to get light, the sun shining in through the window. I needed to leave.

'My da's gone for the doctor. He's gone to see if they'll take you in the hospital until he can think of a better plan. My mam doesn't want you to go,' she told me quietly, looking over her shoulder as if she didn't want to be heard. 'I 'member you now. I was sick and saw your face. Mam says you saved my life. *Not going to die, are you?*' she asked without any sympathy or tact. I shook my head.

'No, I'm not going to die.'

I was not going to die here, in this village. I was not going to die and join my mother on the wrong side of the church wall.

She carried on talking to me, as if we were friends now.

'My cat is fat. She's got babies in there. She's having kittens. I like kittens. Do you like kittens?' She stopped chattering as her mother came back into the room, shifting the child out of the way with her hip. I can see the cat isn't the only one expecting, but say nothing. Now isn't the time. She'll find out soon enough.

'Thomas has gone to see if they've a bed for you in the hospital. Get you better, make you right until we can work out what to do,' she explained.

I started to head to the door, but she stopped me. She put her hand on my arm and guided me to a chair at the table.

'Away now, Caitlin, away and find y'dolly. Go on.' She

170

tried to get rid of the child, to send her out of the room, but she wouldn't go. She stood still, watching, as if she wasn't sure what to make of me.

'Now, pet, wait a while, don't go yet. Let us help you. Is there anyone I can send for? Where's your kin? Where's your mam? Y'must have family somewhere, pet.'

'No,' I replied, not willing to explain about my mother's family and that I was on my way to them, that I was trying to help myself, if only they'd let me go.

'Oh, wee pet, is there no one? I'm so sorry, I should have done more t'help you. I should have come and seen you, but it's no' easy is it, eh? It's no' easy living here with everyone watching your every move. I know what it's like t'be an outsider, see. But still, I should hae come to see you.' She sounded cross with herself, as if she could have changed what happened, as if she could have made a difference. It wasn't her fault.

The door to the cottage burst open and several people came in, some in white, others in black, the farrier behind them. There were voices and shouts and two people pulled me roughly out of the chair. The farrier's wife stood back, looking unsure. She started to argue with her husband again.

'Can it no'wait a while, Thomas?' she pleaded. He shook his head, moving out of the way.

'Can we come and see him at least, pay a visit?' She turned to the men in white, appealing to them.

'Sorry, Missus, sorry. No visitors to the workhouse.' They escorted me to the door. She reached out to me. Her husband pulled her back.

'That's enough now, Aileen. You've done your best by the boy, time to let him go,' he said, soft and firm. She tried to argue with him, but he silenced her by holding the door open.

'Thank you,' I told them. I didn't know what else to say. I caught sight of the little girl, tucked behind her mother, hiding in her skirts. She smiled at me, took her thumb out of her mouth, and tottered over to me, whispering in my ear.

'Come back and see my cat but wait till she's had the kittens,' she instructed me.

'I will and I'll come back to see the baby too,' I whispered back as she pressed a small damp kiss on my cheek before being scooped up by her father. I walked out of the farrier's cottage under guard. I knew that the long road I'd travelled down before lay ahead and at the end of it waited the heavy locked doors to the workhouse.

CHAPTER 29
NOAH

I crane my neck, feeling the new weight of Beth's stone bouncing against my skin as I run along the river path. I didn't even ask Dad if he wanted to come, not after yesterday. Maybe it's better if I just go on my own from now on. We're barely speaking to each other. I skived off school, pretending I had a stomach bug, and spent the day in bed, bored out of my mind with brainless daytime telly for company. Anything not to draw. I convinced Mum a run would do me good, bit of fresh air and all of that. She didn't put up much of a fight; I think she was glad to get me out of the house.

I look up through the ash trees and watch a bat twist and turn, flying very close then slowing and hovering, waiting for something. I am baking and want to jump in the river and cool down. Now I've thought of it, I can't resist. It is too hot to run, especially on my own. I look around, but can't see anyone other than the bat. The rapids thrash away endlessly, there's the odd fish darting past, but no walkers, no other swimmers. I peel off my running shorts and sweaty T-shirt and wade in.

The water is icy despite the hot day as I plunge under,

the coldness throbbing against my scalp. I keep far away from the rapids and stay by the rocks to start with. I let my feet go numb and blue. Once I've swum a few strokes, I start to drift across to the little island in the middle of the river.

I float on my back, letting the waves creep around my neck and into my ears. All sounds switch off. My ears tune in to the pulsing of the river and fade out the noise of the birds, the cars and the rest of the world. I have no idea what time it is or how long I've been in the river, I don't really know what I'm doing, but I tell myself: only a few more minutes, just a little while longer, as the skies darken and the sounds and shape of the river change.

I slip into something, the way I slip into dark places when I'm drawing, but there are no pens or papers here. My eyelids get heavy, weighed down as if someone had placed coins on them. I can't keep them open. My head droops to the side and cold water fills my ear, laps over my lips and nose, gaining in momentum, climbing higher. A high-pitched sound pierces through my eardrum, like a shrill whistle. I feel my mind and my body separate as I sink down into the dark water.

The river chokes my nostrils, fills my throat and makes its way down and down. I know I have to get out. There isn't enough air in my lungs and the water will win. I am so slow. My legs won't work and my toes clamp together in painful spasms. This is new: terrifying and completely out of control.

My eyes open wide underwater. I can see flailing limbs, sinewy arms and bony fingers full of panic, writhing in front of me. There are things here with me, under the water, pulling at me, clawing and scratching at my calves, dragging me down with them, as if I'm bound or tied by ropes. Jagged nails tear into my skin, clutch at my forearms, shoving my shoulders down, deeper and deeper down. Weeds, long and thin like green hair, whirl in front of my eyes. I hear their whispering as the weeds swim past, pleading with me to help them. I try to push them away, but their watery fingers coil around my wrists and ankles like grass snakes.

I have to get back to the surface.

I must get away.

I need air.

Then a hand appears. A different one, stronger, darker.

The solid fingers force their way through the wall of weeds and the hair.

And then everything stops, even the whispering.

I reach out for the hand, but it isn't attached to anyone.

It starts moving, convulsing, almost as if it is trying to tell me something. I stop treading water and watch as the hand opens up and begins to move towards the surface, beckoning me. The skin is puckered, the veins underneath raised up. They look discoloured, almost dead. The hand traces the beams of sunlight that filter down, following them like a map, and I reach out too. I try to grab hold of the hand, desperate to keep it with me, clutching at it, but it twists and then it folds into a fist, charging into my face with full force.

I am out of the water, but I can't remember how I made it to the bank. I am soaking wet, there's blood on my hands and my legs ache. I can't remember anything. I start to panic, cough and then retch.

'You nearly drowned. I had to jump in and rescue you. You panicked,' says a young man, also wet, sitting on the bank next to me, his jeans soaked through. A woman rubs his shoulders, holding a barking liver-and-white spaniel on a red lead. The dog is desperately pulling the woman towards me.

'Stop it, Sammy, just sit! Wait! Ben tried to lift you out of the water, but you kept struggling against him.' The woman is being pulled around by the dog. It barks wildly. She takes her purple hoodie off and wraps it round my shoulders. She shivers, her arms covered in goosebumps.

'He had to knock you out. To stop you from drowning the pair of you! Happens all the time with swimmers. You hear about them getting out of their depth, getting confused and then lashing out.' She tells me with pride how her boyfriend saved me.

I look across at him and he smiles, shrugs his shoulders as if in apology for punching me.

'To be honest I hadn't seen you. It was Sammy here. He

nearly ripped my arm off pulling me down to the water. I kept whistling for him to come back but he wouldn't listen. He knew something was up. Good dog, aren't you, mate? Good boy, Sammy.' He pats the dog's head and rubs his ears. The dog's tail starts up enthusiastically, enjoying the fuss and attention.

I take off the hoodie and give it back to the woman, then stand up unsteadily. I pull my clothes back on as quickly as possible. I am embarrassed, sitting there in my underwear in front of these strangers. Ungratefully, I wish they would leave me be.

'Let us take you home. Come on, you're in a right state.' The boyfriend holds out a hand to me. But I don't want to touch anyone. My skin stings, as if I've spent the day at the beach and got sunburned. I fling my arm out to avoid touching him, shouting, 'Leave me alone!' which makes the girlfriend jump back as if I've hit her. She goes flying over the dog, landing awkwardly on the ground. The dog starts barking again, first at me and then at the man who is now shouting.

'*Bloody hell!*' He helps his girlfriend to her feet and checks to see if I've hurt her, if I've hit her. He shakes his head aggressively at me. It is such a mess. Not quite the response they were expecting for an act of bravery. I feel bad, but the feeling is overwhelmed by how much I need to get away. From them, the river and whatever just happened. For once I want my parents, but not while I'm in this state. I can't risk these two telling all this to my parents, or anyone else.

I run, without any walking or warm-up. I shout sorry as I run past them, head down, my soaked clothes scratching and chafing against my damp, sore, cold skin. I push myself on as hard as I can, as if the man or his dog will try to catch me. I run nearly all the way home, not looking back, not daring to see who might be running after me.

I wake up in my bed. I look across at my clock; the neon numbers glow too brightly in the dark. 23:01. Mum put me there, like a child, after I'd taken a hot shower. I let her fuss over me and I just sat there, on the edge of my bed, waiting for her to leave. She looked so pleased to be looking after me. She is able to love me so easily. I'd fallen asleep quickly, but now I'm wide awake.

I can hear my parents moving around in the hallway, back and forth between the airing cupboard and their bedroom. My bedroom door is ajar. Clearly Mum has been checking on me. In hushed voices they whisper.

'What on earth was he doing, Sadie? What the *hell* was he trying to do?' From my dad.

'He's never been a strong swimmer. That's all there is to it. Tired probably from all the running and he wasn't very well, he spent most of the day asleep. You have to go with him from now on, Daniel. It's not safe for him on his own.' From my mum. Then their bedroom door clicks shut.

I wait for an hour, to make sure they've gone to sleep, then creep down the stairs. I don't know how long I have, but I've already looked everywhere in my room and found nothing. Mum and Dad have cleared the house of all my art stuff while I slept. There is nothing left to draw with. I guess they felt they had to do something after what happened in the river, though I haven't told them the half of it.

All the pens in the house have disappeared. I find the pen pot in the dishwasher. It still has black and blue stains all over it. In the study, the printer is disconnected and empty of paper. I look everywhere, getting more panicked and breathless. I wrench open the 'drawer of doom', usually so full of paper, takeaway menus, junk mail, letters from school, leaflets, lists for shopping and Post-its that you could barely get it open. Now it is full of neatly ironed napkins with napkin rings sitting next to them. We don't use napkins, not unless someone comes for a meal, which is almost never.

I try to find the magazine rack, thinking there'll be something in there, but that has disappeared too. The house feels too clean and empty, like it has been taken away and replaced with a shiny new one that I don't know. I am scared of what's happening, where it might go – as if nearly drowning isn't bad enough. I really want to stop. But I can't. I'm like a *junkie*.

I feel more and more desperate as I pull things out of

179

drawers, fling open cupboards, pull books off shelves, hoping for a bookmark, or an old envelope I can use. I see Mum's handbag on the kitchen table. I unzip it slowly, feeling like a thief. I look over my shoulder, listening for footsteps down the stairs. I know there will be a notebook in her bag somewhere.

I find a brown paper bag with *Flynn's Remedies* printed on the front. I open the bag, even though I'm wasting time. Inside is a small green bottle. It has the tiniest label on it. *Chamomile powder*. Some herbal remedy for something. Mum isn't a fan of doctors and hospitals, doesn't trust them. I heard her tell Dad that going to see the herbalist meant she was '*in the driver's seat, back in charge and taking control*'. Whatever she needed to take control of.

I screw the bag of herbs back up, shoving it near the bottom, out of my sight. I find a brightly coloured notebook with tesselations on. The bold patterns scattered across the front are the kind that gave me headaches, they look like tiles from a mosque. It was in the zipped section of her bag, a smaller compartment you might miss unless you were really looking. The notebook is only half-full of her neat handwriting.

I don't stop to read what she's written. It's bad enough that I am in her handbag going through her stuff. I have to decide whether to take the whole notebook or just rip a few pages out. She won't notice a few missing pages, but she'll definitely be on to me if her whole notebook walks off. I try to take care as I rip out two pages and then shove them in my back pocket. There's a leaky biro in the bottom of her handbag, a small blue stubby one that looks near its end. I take that too.

I come to in the early hours of the morning, my head resting on my hand, as if I'd just fallen asleep at my desk. I have pins and needles and my head is tight. My left hand is twitching and flexing and I feel cold. My hand starts moving again, separate from the rest of my body, searching for something. I lurch forwards and grab my jeans, which are lying on the floor. My eyes are half-shut and heavy, as if I can't open them properly yet. My hand is frantically searching through all the jeans' pockets until it finds the two small squares of paper torn from my mum's notebook. They're so small I wonder what on earth I can draw on them. My brain, arms, legs and hands are fighting against one another. The blue biro fits neatly into the palm of my left hand while my right hand locates the small scraps of paper, blank squares waiting to be filled.

My hand skims across the page, making a mesh of all kinds of blues – light blue, dark blue and blue scribbled so hard it tears through the paper. There's wind and water and no light. Everything in the picture feels like it is in motion, but it's also secretive, hiding something from me in the dark. There's stillness at the centre, a depth that holds something I can't comprehend yet. Underneath the hard scribbled layers rests a hard ledge. A naked foot, all bony and sharp, is balancing on it or falling off it and the toenails are discoloured and unnatural, almost dead-looking.

Wind and water smash down upon it, blurring it and smudging it so that I can't see what's happening. I realise I'm holding my breath as if I'm in there, in the picture, under all the water. I have to make my brain and body work together again or I'll pass out. The panic builds, there's a sharp taste of metal in my mouth and then staleness. I try to swallow, to clear my throat, but it is closing. Air seems to be just out of reach, just above my head as I tilt it up to the light.

How can these flat, two-dimensional images in front of me move, slipping and falling? How can I be sitting in my stuffy room shaking from the bitter cold? I can smell the dankness of rain in a dark place where someone's bones are about to be broken.

I take in a deep breath, as if I'm resurfacing, swimming back up, and then vomit all over the drawings.

CHAPTER 30
BLAZE

I watch the new rain falling as the storm builds. Everything has changed. Yesterday I had my hut, my space, my small treasures, and today I am in a half life. I am not here or there, not one thing or another. In limbo.

I look down at my wrists, marked by the thick knots they'd made when they tied me up. They dragged me to the water like a stray dog. They pushed me down into a dark pool of water. I remember it moving so fast. They tried to kill me, to end me, but I didn't let them.

They were the guilty ones, Emilia and Henry, with their stolen goods and their false tales. But no one would hear me. No one could hear my cries with my head held under the river.

And now all my hope is gone, sinking like my precious stones which they ripped from my throat and the ring that was to be my escape.

I have to find another way.

It can't end here, in this place, not again.

CHAPTER 31
NOAH

I run steadily along the river path towards Beth's house, warming up slowly. I haven't seen her for three days as Mum's kept me off school to 'recover' from what she and Dad have taken to calling the 'incident in the river'. We've been texting, but it isn't the same.

I've missed seeing her face, her hair, her smile, hearing her laugh. I'm keen to get to her house, to make up for lost time, and am just about to step up my pace when something lands on my shoulder. Before I can turn around, something else hits me hard on the back of my skull.

'*Ow!*' I shout, turning around, trainers skidding in the dry mud.

Theo and Eva are following me. Jay, Georgia and Harley run fast to catch them up. As I rub my head, I can see Sam further along the path, hanging back, looking worried. I pull my hand away from my head. It has blood on it. At my feet lies a rock with splashes of red all over it, like spilled paint.

'You've done it now, Theo, look you've made him bleed!' Eva shouts. She pushes Theo nearer to me. He has another rock in his hand and is snarling at me.

'What kind of a freak are you? Like letching on other people's girlfriends, do you, Saunders? Been watching her from your window, have you?' Theo isn't making any sense.

Had she seen me, when I shouted at her? Had she told Theo I'd been watching her? I'll bet she hadn't told him she'd been hanging her brother out of the window.

Eva is holding something behind her back. I'm worried it'll be more rocks. My head is pulsing and sore.

'What do you want, Theo?' I ask, trying to sound bored rather than scared as he and his mates move closer to me.

'You should run to Beth's house, before we tell her what you are. She won't want to know you then. She hasn't got a clue what she's got herself into. This is some serious shit you've pulled … *freak*!' Theo warns, pointing at me. 'We all thought you were into Beth, but turns out we were wrong. Think you know someone, eh? Well, Eva's taken so BACK OFF!'

Theo is shouting now, encouraged by his friends. He pushes me hard towards the edge of the river, moving me away from the path. Eva draws level with me and pulls a sheet of paper from behind her back like a magician. It looks like a worksheet from school.

'How long have you been watching me? How long have you been spying, peeping through your curtains while I get undressed? You sick pervert! I knew you fancied me! I told Beth that you were watching me, but she wouldn't listen.' Eva spits in my face.

185

I wipe it away on the back of my hand, wondering what the hell to do next. I want to shove her away from me.

'Knew you were trouble first day you showed up, looking all cool and calm. Thinking you owned the place. I told her not to trust you. Beth should have run a mile from you. Well, she will now, she'll listen when I show her this!' Eva holds up a crumpled and stained piece of paper covered in my drawings. It's of the back of her house showing her bedroom window and her face in full on close-up detail. I try to grab it, but Eva scrunches up the paper and throws it away from me.

'Too late, Noah. *Too late.* I've seen it and so have Theo and the rest of us, so everyone knows you've been stalking me, watching me through my bedroom window, drawing my face, drawing me smiling when I didn't know you were watching me.'

My stomach drops. I thought I'd got rid of those drawings in our wheelie bin. I remember shoving them down to the bottom, chucking cereal boxes on the top to hide them. How the hell did she find them?

'You should have made sure the lid on your bin was on properly. There was stuff everywhere. Lots of sad little herbal tea boxes and Coco Pops all over the path! I mean who eats Coco Pops still? My dad made me help him put your rubbish back in, moaning on about how the bin men wouldn't take any of the rubbish if there was a mess. And in the middle of your kiddie food, I found all these lovely drawings of me. Didn't know you had such a crush, Noah. It'll be little love letters next!' Eva laughs.

Sam picks up the paper and unfolds it, trying to make sense of what's going on.

'Take a good look at this, Sam, *don't give me that look*, I'm not making it up. See, that's my house there right behind Noah's. That's my bedroom window that this perv has been drawing.' Eva snatches the paper back off Sam and then turns on me.

'What did you do it for?' She thrusts her black pointy nails into my chest. Theo stands next to her in support. He grabs me by my tie and tries to lift me off the ground. Eva's eyes widen but she looks excited rather than surprised. I shout out and Harley and Jay laugh, doing impressions of me. I can see Georgia and Sam looking less sure, turning to see if anyone is coming up the path.

Theo twists the tie around his wrist, pulling it tighter around my neck, choking me as he angles me down towards him. He lets go of my tie suddenly, tipping me off my feet. I fall to the ground, panting desperately, trying to loosen my tie, to get some air.

Before I can get back up, Harley and Jay catch hold of my arms, holding me in place, ready for something. I panic and begin kicking out at them both. I manage to get Harley in the shin hard.

'Shit! C'me here, you.' He rips my shirt sleeve as he gets a tighter hold of my arm, pausing to punch me hard in my ribcage, winding me. I want to cry when they let go of me, unsure what to do next. Theo is arguing with Sam, who keeps on about things getting out of hand, but the distraction technique isn't working.

'Just shut it, Sam! You don't know what's going on here, so just leave your little friend to us, OK?' Theo shouts.

Sam shakes his head, but stands his ground, refusing to leave. I don't have time to call out to him because Eva is hissing at me, talking too fast for me to work out what she's saying. Harley and Jay are now yelling at Sam too, but all I can hear is Eva in my ear as I get to my feet.

'...found the other ones too. You were going to show these drawings to everyone, weren't you? You were going to make them think that I could push my brother out of a window. Was that the plan, Noah?' Eva looks to see if Theo had heard, but he's too busy arguing with Sam, who sounds like he's trying to shut the conversation down.

'You found your tie then?' I spit back and watch her face pale. It feels good for a second. Shutting her up for a moment gives me the chance to think, to work out how to get out of this.

'What are you on about? Anyway, I've got rid of those ones. I *burned* them. So only you and I know what else you drew.'

She is shaken, I can see that, but she's trying to hide it by talking. I picture her little brother hanging out of his bedroom window, his head far over the ledge, and behind him Eva smiling. She isn't smiling now; she looks as if the situation is spiralling out of her control.

'We were just messing around. The windowsill was slippy and I was worried he'd fall. He could have died, you know, I was trying to save him, stupid little idiot. But what you drew is sick, totally out of order!' Eva slaps me hard across my cheek.

'I wasn't going to show them to anyone. I chucked them away, didn't I?' I swore to her.

'For God's sake, just leave it. It's just a couple of pictures, that's all. Go home, Noah!' Sam breaks away from Theo and Harley and shouts at Eva, but she ignores him, leaving Theo to deal with him.

She leans in carefully once more, making sure the others can't hear. 'But it's not just a couple of pictures, is it? How did you *know*? How *could* you have known what was going to happen?' She looks frightened of me. Neither of us knows what to do next, but Theo has been psyching himself back up, enjoying the drama and the scene that's building.

'You're a total freak, drawing my girlfriend and watching her through the window like some creep.' Theo is smiling as he wanders back to me casually, like he's just figured out something that had been bothering him.

'I knew there was something dodgy about you the minute you turned up. I told you, didn't I, Eva? Watch him; he's got his eye on you, he's into you. Arrogant shit thinks he knows it all too.'

Eva had only shown him the pictures of just her, just the close-ups I'd done of her face and not her little brother with her hands around his neck. He didn't know what was really going on here. He couldn't see past the fact that I'd been drawing his girlfriend, looking at his girlfriend. Theo pushes me hard in my chest, wanting to start something. Normally I'd have stepped back, moved away, but something in me sparks and I punch him in his stomach, making him stagger awkwardly into Jay.

Theo recovers quickly. He and Jay both charge at me, knocking me off my feet and over the edge. They'd been herding me towards the water the whole time but I hadn't noticed.

They both jump down after me, thrashing through the shallow water. I get to my feet as they reach me and duck a punch from Theo, aimed at my face. I fling a fist at him, hoping to connect with his nose, knowing this will be painful and delay him for a few minutes, but instead find his bony cheek. Theo falls backwards into the deep water. He rises spluttering, water pouring from his body. He clutches his hand to his face then springs forwards, steadying himself by grabbing the front of my ripped shirt and the skin on my neck. His hand gathers up my necklace as he pulls me in, choking my throat.

'Think you're better than the rest of us, don't you? Well, you're not. You're not like the rest of us. Well, some of us anyway!'

He glares at Sam, who has been shouting at him to stop, and then rips my necklace off and throws it across the river. I watch Beth's stone fly high into the air and then fall into the fast flowing river. He grabs hold of my jaw, snapping my head back to look at his bloodied face as he issues his final warning.

'Stay away from me. Stay away from my girlfriend. And stop drawing her or I'll … report you to the police, *stalker*! You better just watch your back from now on, yeah, cos you never know who'll be watching you.'

I shake him off and try to wade away from him, moving against the current. He thrashes through the water back to the riverbank with difficulty, his sodden clothes weighing him down. Harley holds out a hand and heaves Theo up out of the river.

'Someone's coming!' Sam yells and I wonder if it is true. I don't even care by now. I try to run after Theo, but he's too quick. I stagger back through the water, my trousers clinging to my cold legs. Sam offers a hand but I don't want his help. Eva laughs manically as I pull myself up out of the water. She mutters something about friends to Sam and then runs up the path to catch up Theo and Harley. Georgia shrugs her shoulders at Jay and then follows, trailing after Eva, as always. Sam walks in the opposite direction, away from them and from me. No one is laughing now, or even talking any more. It is so quiet. They walk up the path in silence and around the corner.

CHAPTER 32
BLAZE

I woke in another bed, in a room smelling of piss that had been washed away but lingered still. They told me I was in Halstead Workhouse but I already knew this. I'd been here before. This was the place where Maman and I were sent and where she died. Now the circle was complete, I was back, interred again.

I could feel her presence in the sad air that hovered between the high walls. I remembered them as yellow but the dirt had got to them, staining the paint. I left her here when she died. A woman came and found me, said the Master was entertaining the Guardians, told me to run to Maman while there was still time. I agreed to Maman's last wish, her last right. I promised to leave her, to get out while I could still run.

They told me, 'You're in the infirmary,' as if that should make it better, but I was freezing in an iron bed with a thin grey blanket and no fire or Dog to warm my feet and send me to sleep with his snores. I soaked the bed with my cold sweats and for a long time no one came to help me. Eventually a woman sighed her way into the room, heavy footed and wheezy. She talked while she worked and at first I was not sure if there was someone else in the room or if she was speaking to me. The other beds looked empty but I couldn't be sure.

'You came back then. Well, you're not the only one, don't worry. Hold still … and turn.' She heaved my body and I flipped over. She pulled the damp sheets out from under me with one hand. The other held me up, cold and rough on my back.

'Don't 'spose you remember me, do you? I remember you though, remember your mother too.' She paused to look at me as she tucked a dry sheet under me. She let me go and I dropped back against the narrow bed.

'She was a jacket woman, wasn't she, your mother? They made her wear a yellow jacket when she turned up, because of you.' She pointed her finger at me, as if I was at fault. I didn't understand her. I shook my head just once. I didn't see my mother again once they separated us so I had no idea what clothes she wore. When I saw her for the last time, she was in a bed, like this one, in a white gown.

'Jacket women, unmarried mothers, plenty of us in here. Look at me!' She pointed to her yellow jacket and gave me a sad smile. They must have made them wear clothes to mark them, make them stand out in shame. My stomach turned over in pity for my mother.

'Your mother didn't make much sense to me, but we did manage a few words, now and then. She told me about your father, him being sent away to sea in shame. Always wondered what a gipsy girl like her was doing in these parts. All on her own she was, except for you.' She chattered on as if I knew all of this, as if my mother and I had shared this story, *our story*, many times. I didn't have the strength to tell her the only stories my mother told me were made-up ones.

'She was a good girl though. Selly, we called her, couldn't get my tongue around her funny name, sounded like celery to me! She had her funny ways, said she was a lady's maid or a French maid, but I never really believed her. Didn't seem likely. I told her all about my Minnie when I could and she talked about you. I was sorry to see her go, when she passed.' She stopped tucking the sheet under me, then leans in.

'What did you say?' she asked, her breath warm on my face.

'Céline. Her name was Céline,' I forced out through my cough.

She moved even closer and I recoiled, unsure, but then she wrapped her arms around my shoulders, holding me close for a moment. I felt the cold, hard iron of the bed press against me.

All I needed to do now was wait, watch and wait.

She released me and promised to come back later.

I must have fallen asleep because when I opened my eyes,

the light from the moon rested on the empty beds. I was the only one in here now. The woman bustled around noisily clearing old cups and plates and setting down new ones. I pushed myself up. I felt better. My bones were lighter and I could hear singing as I ate and drank the food she'd brought me.

It was late in the evening as the white moon shone on the brick wall. A nightingale started his evensong and I knew what I had to do. I could wait. I could bide my time, I decided, as I watched the woman moving around the room and the keys that hung from her belt, clanking and clanging in time to the nightingale's chorus.

CHAPTER 33
NOAH

Beth sits on the churchyard wall, swinging her legs, ear-buds in, listening to something. I feel like running to her but manage to keep it together enough to walk across the road. My hand has other ideas as it dances in the air, waving at her, a limb with a mind of its own.

'You're late. Why weren't you in school again yesterday? I tried ringing you but your phone went to answerphone. I feel like I haven't seen you all week,' she tells me, pulling her ear-buds out. Beth jumps down off the wall, picks up her bag and pushes the gate open. I follow her into the churchyard.

'I texted you, I was ill. So where are we going? Why did I have to meet you before school?' I ask, nervous about what Theo might have said to her, or what Eva might have shown her.

'Somewhere private. I want to talk to you.'

She sent me a text last night asking to meet before school but wouldn't tell me why. I wonder if she knows, if she's found out somehow about what happened with Theo or worse, maybe she's found out about Grace. She walks through the damp graveyard purposefully. It is still in shade, slightly dark and very quiet. She runs her hand over the top of a mottled gravestone and closes her eyes for a second.

'What are you doing?' I whisper.

'Saying a prayer for Beloved,' she answers and then pulls a face at me.

'Who's *Beloved*?' I ask.

She laughs softly and points at the headstone.

HERE LIES THE BODY OF THOMAS GARLAND,

BELOVED HUSBAND OF AILEEN GARLAND

AND LOVING FATHER TO

CAITLIN AND THOMAS GARLAND.

There's some more stuff about *taken from this earth* and *something of this parish* that I can't read properly, but I don't get why Beth is so interested in a Garland headstone. Clearly they weren't related.

'Who is he then?' I ask.

'I don't know. It's just something we used to do on the way out from Sunday School. We'd walk past the headstones and pick one. This one, Thomas, was mine because he was *Beloved*. I just loved the word. We'd all touch our headstone, say a little prayer and then run out. Last one to the gate had to go back and touch all three headstones again, *on their own!*'

'Who's we?' I ask, slightly jealous of her playing this

game with someone other than me, wishing that I'd know her all my life.

'Oh … Eva, Georgia and me. We used to go to Sunday school together when we were little. They've both been really odd the last few days. They've stopped talking to me. Both of them were talking about me in the loos at lunch yesterday, but they went silent when I came in.' She looks fed up.

'So what happened?' I prompt, desperate to find out what they might have said, to see if that's what this talk is all about. I have some drawings of Eva in my bag, and the other drawing too, the one with the bones. I should just get them out and show her, tell her all of it, just spit it out, be honest for once and show her what I am, a freak. *A total freak.* I don't need to be tested in the river like a witch. But I don't want her to change the way she feels about me, not now we were back to normal again. So I don't say anything, I sit and wait like a coward.

'I don't know, they were talking about you and me, I think. She won't tell me what I've done. Georgia won't speak to me until Eva does … so. She's been acting like such a diva, such a control freak, since she and Theo got back together again. She came up with a list of rules about what we could wear, how we should look, who we had to fancy a few weeks ago, when you started school actually, and I'm just not into it. I know I've seen less of them since … I met you, but I don't know what I've done to deserve this silent treatment and the nasty texts she's been sending me.' Her voice rises, defensive.

I put my arm around her and she turns into my chest. I feel like a traitor as I wrap both arms all the way around her, cocooning her, as if I can protect her.

Beth loosens my arms, breaking my hold gently and reaches down to pick up her bag.

'She sent another one last night, here, I'll show you; it's a bit weird. It's not bitchy like the others, but there's something mean about it.' She touches Thomas Garland's headstone again and then takes my hand, leading me into the church.

Inside, she drops my hand and takes out her mobile. We sit on the back pew and I read the text she shows me.

> So you think you know someone but turns out
> you can't trust anyone, Beth. Watch your back!
> You never know who might be watching you.

It's a threat not a warning. They must have known she'd show me Theo's words. I bet he got Eva to send it.

'I give up with her. Nothing makes her happy. She's one of those people that has to have some kind of drama going on all the time and if nothing's happening she'll make something happen. I'm just … tired of it. I've had enough,' she tells me before deleting the text. I watch her scroll through her phone to her contacts page and she smiles at me before pressing down hard on the name EVA. She gets a second chance when the screen asks her if she's sure she wants to delete this contact. But she doesn't want a second chance, she thinks this will solve the problem, but I am the problem. I've caused this rift and I have to sort it out, even if it means messing things up between us. She throws the phone down onto the pew.

Beth holds her hand up to the light coming in through the stained-glass windows spattered with rain and then reaches out for my hand. She wraps her fingers around mine, our different skin tones now all the colours of the rainbow together in the church. I have to tell her, now while we're on our own. I am ready to confess and in church is as good a place as any.

'It's my fault, what's going on with Eva and it's not just that, there's something else I have to tell you too, something that happened before…'

I start as her phone's alarm clock beeps the time at her. 8:50am. The phone vibrates manically against the pew and Beth swears, the word out of place echoing round the empty church, as we realise how late we are. She hasn't heard me; she hasn't taken in what I was trying to say.

She grabs her bag, then my hand, and pulls me out of the church and into the rain. The weather has changed in the last few days, unpredictable, sudden heavy rain then back to meltingly hot sun again. We run all the way to school, our hoodies zipped up to the top, ducking our heads to avoid the pelting rain, diving in and out of the puddles on the path. Neither of us wants to miss the bus. We've been told it will leave at 9am 'on the dot'. It's only to the workhouse museum in Halstead for History but at least it was a day out together.

I sit next to Beth on the bus; we are the last ones on, so we have to take seats near the front. We both shake ourselves off before sitting down. I take off my wet hoodie and spread it out on the headrest to dry and Beth does the same. My knees push into the seat in front of me, my soggy thighs pressing up against hers as I try to shoehorn myself into the small space. I hear our names shouted out as we sit down, our backs to everyone apart from the driver, Mr Bourne and Miss Empingham, the other History teacher. I feel uncomfortable, unsure if this is the right time to tell her, but I have to. I have to get in there first before Eva.

Beth starts chatting to me, taking my hand, playing with the calluses on my palm as she raises her voice above the cheers, shouts, teasing and chatting of the class and above the first crack of thunder. I hate storms.

'How did you get these marks on your hand? That one looks like a star,' she asks, running her fingers along them.

'From drawing, I guess.' I watch her small hand flutter over mine. My stomach turns over as I look at the criss-cross of scratches and scars on my hands, remembering the drawing. I want to show it to her. I should have shown her in the church and now it is too late, there's no chance of privacy on the bus. I hear our names called out again, followed by a word hissed down the aisle. It sounded like *freak*s and *bitch* or … possibly *witch*? It sounds like Theo and Harley and definitely Eva too. I can hear high-pitched, forced giggling coming from the back of the bus.

Beth has been staring at my neck. She touches her own necklace and then drops my hand, turning her body away from mine. She focuses out the window, concentrating really hard on the view as her fingers follow the trail of a raindrop. A solid silence descends over us for the rest of the journey. I pull the neckline of my T-shirt up, pointlessly trying to hide the empty space she's just seen, where her necklace and stone should be.

A long tall building greets us as we drive into the car park. It has a ridiculous amount of windows all the same shape and size, rows and rows all lined up like soldiers. It stands to attention, tall, proud and intimidating.

'Here we are, Halstead Workhouse. Take one of these between two as you get off the bus and make your way to the front entrance. No pushing please, take care down the steps.' Mr Bourne and Miss Empingham hand out worksheets, clipboards and pens as we step off the bus relieved that the rain has stopped. Beth stands next to me chewing her pen. I tap her arm and nudge her to get moving and she scowls at me. Great, it's going to be *that* kind of day.

We walk up a long graveled path to the front door; on our left and right are huge vegetable gardens with runner beans, cabbages, onions and carrots all in neat rows, like the windows, uniform and precise. I feel messy just walking along the path, out of place and time. There's a high red brick wall surrounding the building, locking it in, framed by wrought iron gates, dull black doors and neatly squared, leaded windows. It is such a plain building, a tessellation with everything matching and repeated over and over like a child's drawing.

'Now if you were just arriving in the workhouse you would be split up from your family, males and females were kept separate, parents and children divided. They had different sleeping and working quarters and very different jobs. The men on the whole got the worst jobs; bone picking was bottom of the heap as well as stone breaking. The women tended to work in the laundry rooms or plaited straw, were seamstresses or given general cleaning and cooking duties.' As Mr Bourne talks each of us has a turn at the water pump or with the mangle. Beth lifts the handle of the pump but can't get it working. I try but it is freezing cold, despite the heat of the sun.

'They must have disconnected it so kids don't get the yard wet or something,' Beth mutters, watching my useless attempts to get some water in the bucket.

Theo barges into me, knocking me out of the way and takes his turn, yanking the arm of the pump really hard over and over until it looks like he might break it. I smirk, glad that he hasn't got it to work either. He stops and stares at me.

'Funny, is it, yeah? Well, it depends on what you find *freaky*, I guess. Depends on how much you want to push your luck, doesn't it?' He sneers at me and rubs his bruised red cheek. Harley pats him on the shoulder and murmurs something about *'time and place, mate, time and place'*. Beth is kneeling down trying out a mangle with a scrubbing brush; she looks up when she hears Theo snap at me. She gives both of us a death stare this time.

'Suits you, Beth, doing the scrubbing. Do you think that's what you'd have been, a little scrubber in the workhouse?'

Beth flings the brush into the bucket, gets to her feet and marches over to Eva, ready to give her a mouthful for that, but Eva talks right over her, turning to show Beth her back and starting to flirt with Mr Bourne.

'Hey, maybe you should split us up, Sir, like it would have happened in the old days? You know, keep the boys separate from us girls so we can't get up to anything! Cos some people just don't know what or who's good for them! Some people have to be told.' Eva smiles sweetly at Mr Bourne and then points at me and Beth. Georgia forces a laugh, looking anxiously from Eva's fake smile to Beth's furious face, unsure what to do next. Clearly Eva has decided the silent treatment is over and it's time to make some trouble.

'Do you know that's not such a bad idea, Eva? Let's really try to understand what life would have been like here for children *nobody* wanted, you know, complete rejects,' Beth fires back.

'Yes, well done, Eva!' Mr Bourne cuts in, sensing the tension between the girls. He organises us into single-sex groups. I get dumped with Theo, Harley and Sam as Beth is herded into the kitchens with Georgia and Eva.

The sun hides behind a cloud and I shiver, feeling the drop in temperature right down to my feet. I look down and see water splashing over my baseball boots. It is gushing out of the water pump, flowing out into the yard. Theo has got the water pump working and has angled it to flow over my feet just as the rain starts hammering down again. He and Harley laugh, punching each other on the shoulder. They hover by the water pump watching everyone else file out of the courtyard, but don't follow. Harley has something behind his back. Theo moves in front of him to shield him from view. They see me watching and stop laughing. Their silence echoes around the almost empty courtyard. I can smell the storm coming, there's a tang in the air. I look across at Sam, who smiles carefully and waves his hand towards the doors. I follow him, trying really hard not to stop or turn around to see what they are up to. I don't want to give them the satisfaction.

Upstairs in the dormitories are beds that look like they belong in a hospital with grey woollen sheets over them, white chamber pots underneath. Next to each bed is a peg halfway up the wall. Again it is like a tessellation, patterns repeated without any variation, colour or warmth. The windows are huge and let in a lot of light but it still feels dark to me.

I am heavy inside, heavy and low standing there imagining what it would have been like. It isn't just the company of Theo and Harley that's getting to me, it's the place. It is so cold, empty and soulless. In each room are information boards with old photos, records, lists of admittances, family histories and case studies. There are a lot of people from Sible Hedingham, so the work Mr Bourne had set us isn't exactly challenging.

Theo sneers, 'Let's go down into the kitchens. It says here that a bunch of people from the village ended up down there, there's a woman who used to work in The Swan and another bloke who was her husband and … oh, look at this, an *imbecile*! This is bang out of order. Seriously *rude*! Can you imagine that, Sam, being called a perv or freak? Hey, Noah, wonder what they'd have put next to your name? Liar, spy, or just *village idiot*?'

My temper flares and I'm halfway across the room

before I've had a chance to think anything through. I push him hard in the chest, making sure I stand tall over him. Sam hovers next to me, worried I'll hit Theo again, but by this point I'm past caring.

'I don't know what your problem is but leave me and Beth out of it,' I tell Theo.

'Let's just go, Noah.' Sam tries to get me out of there.

'Yeah? Got something to hide from Beth, have you Noah? I'm guessing you're not the only one either. We've all got our little secrets, haven't we, Sam?' Theo leers at me, his voice too confident as he swaggers towards Sam.

'Whatever, Theo. I'm going down to the kitchens. You coming, Noah?' Sam says, trying hard to ignore Theo's comments.

'You can stay up here if you like, talking about imbeciles – you're in good company.' I point at Harley, no longer caring how they'll take it. I follow Sam out of the room, but Theo grabs the back of my shirt, pulling me off my feet. I hear the material rip as Mr Bourne walks into the room, slamming the door behind him.

'*What-the-hell-is-going-on-in-here?*' he hisses at us, making each word louder and angrier than the rest. He looks around him in disbelief. 'Noah, get up off the floor now; give him a hand up, Sam. Theo and Harley, go and find Miss Empingham's group. GO! Noah, you can come with me and the girls, you too, Sam.' He holds his hand up as if to say no argument.

I am delighted, I'd much rather be with the girls. I grin at Theo and Harley as they are sent out of the room. I stick two fingers up at them, making sure Mr Bourne doesn't see me. Sam puts his hand over his mouth to cover his laughter as we follow Mr Bourne out of the dormitory and down the stairs to the kitchen where he's left the girls. So many feet have gone up and down them that the stairs are worn in the middle, making them very uneven. There's little light so I go slowly, taking care not to fall into the back of Sam. I'm not in a hurry to get to the kitchens; there's a damp smell coming up the stairs. Something lingers in the air, weighing me down. I nearly lose my footing on the sharp ledge of the last step.

CHAPTER 34
BLAZE

When she left this time, taking my soup bowl and cup with her, I followed her out. The corridors were empty, silent and long. Everyone else must be asleep. I waited for her to go down the stairs first and stepped lightly after her. She walked slowly down the passageway into the kitchens. I hid in the storage areas when she stopped to rub at her back. She kept going, all the way down into the dark basement. She placed the bowl and cup in the large enamel sink and sat down heavily in a chair at the table. We were alone. I folded myself up into a crevice in the wall, full of bags of clean straw, and waited.

She didn't take long to fall asleep; her snoring was soon steady and even. I untangled my legs and trod lightly across the floor; her back was to me so I couldn't see her face but her shoulders rose and fell as her snoring grew stronger. I knelt down at her skirts and looked for the keys that hung from her belt – I didn't touch her yet, I didn't want to risk waking her. The ring holding the keys was large and heavy looking, there were so many keys, and I didn't know which one I needed so I had to take them all. I tentatively touched the hook with my fingers, it was cold and hard. My thumb and first finger pinched and pushed to undo the catch on her belt. But it wouldn't move. I pushed at it again but it was stuck.

I spotted a pat of butter uncovered on the table and rubbed my fingers in it, then smeared some around the catch, hoping to loosen it. The grease worked and it fell away from the belt into my hand. I clasped my fingers around the keys to stop them clanging against one another. I stayed crouched and silent a moment longer, expecting her to wake, to grab my hand and call for help. But she didn't, she simply slept on.

I walked through the outer kitchens and the cold storerooms and felt the temperature dip as I reached the great oak door to the long tunnel. There were too many keys. I searched by size, imagining a door this big will match a large key. I tried three before I got the right one. The lock turned, I pushed the door open and stepped through into the corpse tunnel.

I had been in here before, watching as they rolled the cart along, piled high with bodies, bones and limbs, my mother's body in there somewhere. I held my breath tight in my mouth as they loaded the bodies onto a waiting cart and horse. But there was no one down here now, no men passing the dead out into the night, taking them off to be buried on the wrong side of the church wall. Tonight it was just me and all the sad souls who had travelled through this tunnel under the cover of darkness.

I was not afraid.

I had nothing to fear from the dead and more to fear from the living and that pushed me on. That knowledge drove me along the wet and cold tunnel lit only by the moon flooding in through the grates. The drip, drip, drip of the rain kept a steady beat and I marched to it. I marched towards the great rounded door at the end and knew that this was the only way out. I just hoped I had the key that would set me free.

CHAPTER 35
NOAH

'These long narrow passageways leading off the kitchen were the brewery tunnels. You see, they gave beer to the inmates with most meals, even the children. I know, it must seem very strange to your generation but beer was cheaper than tea, which was regarded as a treat or luxury. It was given to the older women sometimes, but more often than not to the sick and infirm.' Mr Bourne points along the thin tunnel that seems to have no end in sight. People are grouped together in threes and fours as we walk along the brick floor which has water trickling down from the low walls and curved roof. The storm must have broken.

There are small stores off to the left all along the tunnel with empty barrels to show us what it would have looked like. I take Beth's hand in the dark, knowing we'll be unseen, and after a few seconds' hesitation she wraps her fingers around mine. Eva and Georgia are in front with Mr Bourne and some other girls. Mr Bourne is stooping to avoid hitting his head on the roof. I concentrate on doing the same. Eva carries on taking centre stage asking Mr Bourne question after question, doing a good job of pretending to be interested, *the model student*.

'So what else were these tunnels used for then, Sir? It said in the records room upstairs that the tunnels had more than one use. Beth said that some people from our village used them for deliveries or maybe it was smuggling! Beth's really good at spotting stuff like that, you know, little secrets people like to keep,' Eva presses on, turning around to smile sweetly at us.

Beth looks up at me, shaking her head. 'I didn't say anything in the records room. I don't know what she's up to.' I squeeze her hand tighter and pull her a little bit closer to me. This time she doesn't move away.

'Well, that's a good observation. These tunnels did, in fact, have another use; I'm surprised you spotted that, well done, Beth. These tunnels were also known as corpse tunnels. I'm sure you can guess who passed through them from the name. *The dead.* They would be carried on little wooden boards with wheels underneath, like a cart or a trolley, I suppose. They would be pushed to the end of the tunnel and either carried up the steps or passed through the big door at the end to be delivered to a waiting carriage or cart.' Mr Bourne shares this information slowly, as if he isn't sure he should be giving us all the gory details.

'Why were they taken out through an underground tunnel?' I ask, curious about the secrecy.

'Because the Masters didn't want anyone to see.' Mr Bourne is being cagey now and tries to talk over my next question, but I don't let him.

'See what? What didn't they want people to see?' I drop Beth's hand, feeling panicked. There isn't enough fresh air and water keeps dripping on my head as we walk along the long tunnel.

'The bodies. And the bones. You see paupers had no rights, not even to their own bodies. After they died, their bodies had to be paid for by family so they could be buried.' He peers at his watch, muttering something about lunchtime.

'What about those without families? What happened to them?' Beth asks in a quiet voice, moving closer to me again, slipping her small hand back into mine.

'Well … in some cases their bodies were given over to science,' Mr. Bourne replies, keeping his answers as sketchy as possible.

'"Given over to science"? Are you talking in code, Sir? This is a field trip, isn't it? Shouldn't you be telling us *everything*?' Eva joins in, moving to stand too close to Mr Bourne in the almost dark.

'They were sent away to be dissected. They'd be cut up into pieces so that medical students could learn about the different parts of the body. That's right isn't it, Sir? The Masters sold off the bodies and bones to science and pocketed the cash.' Sam surprises us all, his voice ringing out with knowledge, clashing with Mr Bourne's awkward silence.

'Erm … sadly yes, Sam. So that's why this tunnel is

called a corpse tunnel because the bodies would be secretly taken out of this tunnel and away to be … used.' Mr Bourne sighs, realising that he isn't going to be able to shut us up now. He must have remembered how fascinated most of the class had been with the gory details about witches being ducked and swum in the river. He looks like he is regretting ever bringing us down here, into these corpse tunnels, and he isn't the only one. I really want to leave and wish they'd all just shut up.

'What happened then?' Beth asks, her arm pressing against mine.

'The bones might return here to be disposed of in the workhouse grounds or possibly in a field near a church, as close to holy ground as they could get. But they wouldn't be given a proper burial. Often their name would be chalked on the coffin but would have worn off by the time it was buried, so no one even knew who was in there,' Sam replies. 'This meant that their soul would be stuck in purgatory, didn't it, Sir, in limbo? The afterlife was really important, wasn't it, Sir, back then in the Victorian times? That's why people tried to raise money to buy back the dead bodies, but lots just couldn't afford it. I read a book about it, *My Life as a Pauper in the Workhouse*.' He finishes.

'*Oh yes!* Do you remember that archaeologist Miss Empingham got in last year when they found the bones in the field next to St Peter's? Remember, Beth, you had all those nightmares 'cos it's the field behind your house.

Whoooo! The bones, the pauper bones are coming to get you and knock at your window!' Georgia looks proudly at Eva as she teases Beth, half joking, half serious. Both Beth and Sam stare her down which eventually shuts her up.

'Do you remember that poem he taught us? *"Rattle his bones over the stones; he's only a pauper who nobody owns. Rattle his bones over the stones; he's only a pauper who nobody owns,"* Eva sings out loud in the tunnel, her shrill voice ricocheting off the damp walls. Mr Bourne frowns at both Eva and Georgia but before he can say anything Beth starts shouting her voice made bolder by the acoustics in the tunnel.

'Why do you do that? Why do you keep on pushing, Eva? What's the matter with you? This isn't funny, this isn't another joke. You've got no respect, all you care about is yourself and I'm sick of it … *I'm sick of you!*' Beth tells her and opens her mouth to carry on but Mr Bourne steps in front of Beth, turns his back on her and snaps at Eva and Georgia talking over Beth in a loud and sarcastic voice, the kind of voice he saves up in the classroom only bringing it out when someone's really pushed him to the edge.

'Well, Eva and Georgia, seeing as you know so much about this, you can write up some notes and perhaps after lunch the two of you can give a little lecture to the rest of the class, as you both like talking and singing so much. Now walk!' He guides them in front of him, marching forwards to avoid any more exchanges or arguments. Sam looks from me to Beth, backs away and breaks into a jog to catch Mr Bourne up, their heads lean in to one another as they walk along the narrow tunnel towards the end. I can hear snatches of their conversation, the topic of corpse tunnels capturing both their imaginations.

I turn to Beth, just able to make out her face in the light coming from the open sun holes in the tunnel roof; the rain has stopped again. She's trying hard not to cry. I put my arm around her.

'Just ignore them; they're a pair of little witches. You don't need them, honestly,' I try to reassure her.

'It's not that, Noah. I don't care about them; they're not even my real friends anymore. It's here that's freaking me out, what happened in this tunnel!' She pushes me away. I am confused.

'Those poor people who came through here, just a heap of decaying bodies on an old cart going off to be hacked to pieces, for science! They were made of flesh and bones, just like you and me. And no one cared about them, or had the money to save them; no one bought their bodies back home to bury them properly. No one even knew who was in the coffin, just a box of bones. It's just awful, *so so sad*.' We both look around the tunnel, imagining the carts being pushed past us. I try hard not to shiver as she starts again.

'No one would have stood and prayed over them like they should, to say goodbye or help them on their journey into the next life. My mum's family don't see death as the end of life but the start of another. In Vietnamese culture we believe that the family has an obligation to the dead, to make things right and that wasn't allowed to happen here! There's no respect or honour and I just can't stop thinking about all those poor souls trapped somewhere in… What did Sam call it?' She stumbles over her words.

'Limbo,' I answer quietly. She's right; it is desperate. What a hideous way to end your life, being stolen down an underground tunnel, your body bought and then returned as a bag of bones bouncing along these bricks on the back of a cart. A Corpse Tunnel, the name suits the place. I want to get out, I need to leave now and take Beth with me.

'Let's just get out of here, let's run to the end!' I blurt out, wanting to take Beth into the daylight. She's worrying me; she isn't acting like herself going on about limbo and death. I look up the tunnel and can just see Eva and Georgia's backs as they turn the corner following the others out. I take her arm to follow them, but she won't move.

'Where's my necklace? The one I gave you with the special stone?' she asks, standing in front of me, blocking my way.

'I lost it. I'm sorry. I was going to tell you.' My words tumble out, sounding vacant and limp. I try to take her hand again, but she shakes me off.

'You *lost* it? Lost it how and when? I told you it was special.' She places her hands on hips, waiting for an answer. She looks hurt but angry too and I know there's no easy way out of this.

'Um … I think I lost it yesterday or the day before maybe. I can't remember. I'm so sorry, I know it's special.' I'm embarrassed, remembering how Theo ripped it from my neck.

'What are you not telling me, Noah?' she asks and I count up all the secrets I'm keeping from her and wonder where to start.

'I told you not to give it to me,' I whisper instead, my hand going to my empty neck, where her stone should be.

'Well … that's a little bit shit, isn't it?' she snaps at me and marches off down the tunnel into the darkness.

'Wait! Beth, *wait?*'

But she's started running now, away from me. I run to catch her up, she could easily slip and fall in here, it is so damp. She reaches the end of the tunnel, ready to turn the corner; we are the only ones left. All the others must have already climbed the sharp flight of steps in front of us. The big door looks locked and bolted. The steps must lead back up into the courtyard. I can't wait to get us both out of there. I hear Beth panting, short and sharp, as she stops to catch her breath.

'After you,' she snaps, still refusing to look at me. I move past Beth, running up the first few steps, trying to get out, to get some air. My head is getting tight; a buzzing in my temples makes it hard to focus. All I can think is that when we get to the top, I'll tell her. I decide, I'll tell her everything then. I look at the steps in front of me then close my eyes. I've captured every scratch and dip and curve of the stone with my pencil. I know before I open my eyes, before I even have the chance to count them exactly how many steps it will take to get us to the top.

Then I hear it, the drop and fall of something behind me down in the tunnel.

I smell the water before I see it, stale and stagnant. I turn around and see Beth about to lose her balance on the bottom step, her mouth hanging open in surprise as the sound of wood cracking and splintering fills the narrow tunnel. In less than a second everything is in motion, water charging, white crested waves of foam and movement so fast I can't make sense of it. I see her blue flip-flops fly off her feet as a torrent of water knocks her over. She screams and disappears underneath the dark water. I hear a crack, something smashing and breaking, followed by her hollow howl as she tries to push her way up. I spin too quickly on my ankle, which becomes numb with painful pins and needles. Instead of jumping down the steps to Beth, I slip and fall on top of her in a heavy heap as the old door at the end of the tunnel shatters, finally giving way to the force.

Bits of wood are in the air and under the water,

smashing into the walls and off the roof. Splinters fly past our heads as we duck under the black water together. It's like a river out of control. I pull Beth up and out of the water by her arms. I try to stand her up but she just keeps screaming, her leg folding underneath her threatening to plunge her back into the water and the debris. I can just about hear her roaring in pain under the rush of the water. I have to get her out but both of us are struggling to stand. My legs are shaking, spasms running up and down my thighs which are freezing and useless. The water is coming down the steps from above as well as through the old doorway, all charging along the tunnel we came down.

I can see we won't be able to make it out that way; I am going to have to climb the steps which are somewhere underneath the waterfall. I manage to stand for a moment, my feet planted wide apart, and lift Beth up into my arms. She squirms and writhes in pain, her long black hair lying across her face. She's clinging to my neck, almost choking me. There's a big cut on the side of her head running with blood.

And the water keeps rising.

I place my foot on the first step and heave myself up. I lift my legs awkwardly in the fast water. Beth is small but her clothes are wet and she feels heavy in my arms. As I climb the second step the sharp ledge cuts through my soggy baseball boots. Beth must have passed out, her eyes are now closed. I don't know if I am holding her right. I don't know what she's broken. The pain must be coming from a broken ankle or leg looking at the weird position she's in. Her hands are hanging lifelessly behind my neck; I need to wake her up. I try to talk to her, to keep her conscious, but I can barely get the words out as I stagger up the next three steps trying to stay away from the uneven stone wall. The flow of the water seems to be focused on the middle of the steps like a jet stream. My jeans are soaking, getting heavy very quickly, dragging me down and I nearly lose my balance as my torn boots slip again on the sharp steps. The ledge is uneven and doesn't dip in the middle as the other steps had; it dips all over the place. I push back against the water which keeps pushing us dangerously close to the jagged wall. I can't steady myself as I hold Beth tightly with one arm balancing her weight on my thighs. I'm going to fall and take her down with me. My muscles strain as I start to slide off the step. She's making whimpering noises but her eyes stay closed, her arms hanging so loosely around my neck. I need her to hold on but she can't. My thighs convulse as I slip. I reach out with my left hand to try and stop the inevitable, or at least break our fall. I search in the freezing water for the edge of the step that I know is here. My fingers scrape against something at last connecting with the stone and I feel the solid mass underneath my feet and I tell myself to count.

A breath in is one step.

CHAPTER 36
BLAZE

None of the keys worked, they were all the wrong shape and size. I turned to go up the steps, knowing there was another door at the top and hopefully another way out, like last time, but the great big door clicked and cracked, making me jump back up the steps catching my shin on the hard stone. I silenced my cry of pain and felt my leg weep with blood. The large door fell open to reveal a man. There was nowhere to hide, but even so, I covered my mouth, quietened myself and waited.

And watched.

And waited.

The man tried to push a cart through the door and paused, looking up the tunnel for help; it was too heavy for one man. He held a lantern up and then saw me, crouching on the steps.

'*Good God!* Who are you? What are you doing up there?' he asked. I said nothing because I knew who he was. I'd seen him before in my drawings. I'd drawn him swimming up to the surface, I *knew* this man and I knew his sister. He was the sailor, the only survivor. And now it was my turn to survive, to swim up to the surface and find my way out and with the keys in his hand he would show me the way.

'Are you the latchkey lad?' he asked, looking past me for someone else, someone with the answers.

'Yes,' I replied without hesitation.

'Good, then take hold of this cart and help me pull it in, quick now before someone spots us. Come on now, they're waiting out there.' He reached out his hand to me and pulled me up off the step.

'Don't want the horses to alert anyone, do we?' he asked looking over his shoulder through the open door into the tunnel. I did as I was told and helped the man pull the long wooden cart all the way into the tunnel. When we were done he stopped, hands on his knees and caught his breath before pulling the door shut behind him.

'We're late getting back tonight. Shipping them they are, over the sea. Bit of a change to the usual order, eh?' I had no idea what he was talking about but nodded confidently.

'You new then?' He looked me up and down, sizing me up.

'Yes,' I replied, trying to say as little as possible.

'Where's the other lad?' he asked. I shrugged my shoulders, as if I didn't care one way or the other.

'Well, I suppose you'll do as well as him. Are you coming with us then? I said I'd bring a lad or two onto the boat with me. You can learn the ropes, better than staying in this place, eh?' He started walking towards the door, stopping only to look at me again.

'Yes.' I said, trying to stand taller, look stronger and able. 'Yes, I'm coming.' He nodded, rubbing the sweat away from his forehead and pushed a cap down low.

'What's your name then, latchkey?' he asked.

'Blaze,' I replied, telling the truth for the first time.

'Haven't heard that one before. Well, I'm Daniel. Daniel White but you can call me Dan; everyone does, except for my sister Jenny. Come on then, quick. We've got a few hours left before the ship sails, we'll need to change the horses too, I should think. Are you in or are you out?' He saw my uncertainty.

'Where are we going? I mean where are we sailing to, Daniel?' I tried to lower my voice, to fit in with his image of me, trying to say his name as if he were a complete stranger.

'France o'course. Don't they tell you anything in here? I thought you were a seafaring lad, that's what they promised, a seafaring lad who wouldn't be seasick, not like the last one we had. Good job he wasn't on the boat with me afore that because that didn't end well. Not to worry lad, not to worry I'm sure we'll be fine this time, no more earthquakes I promise and a better boat I have never seen, just the right size for the cargo we'll be carrying.' He nudged me as if I was in on the joke. I smiled.

'Corpse cargo! Ah don't mind me, I find it easier to have

a bit of gallows humour about this work. Those new schools over there want some of our English bones, brains and bodies to do their studies on. Come on now, lad, you have to laugh, else you'd cry. I don't ask no questions mind and neither should you. Keep this shut and those open and you'll be fine.' He laughed at me, pointing at my mouth and eyes.

'So, what's it to be, Blaze boy, are you ready for a bit of adventure?' he asked me one last time as he heaved his weight against the great door and pushed hard to open it.

'Yes I am,' I answered stepping outside. I looked across at the snorting horses and the steam from their nostrils in the cold night air, they were attached to a large cart and two men were pulling sheeting of some kind over awkward shapes and tying it down with rope. A corpse cart. We'd all heard the rumours about them and the comings and goings in the tunnels at night. He turned to shut the corpse tunnel away, twisted the key in the lock then pocketed it.

'Good, good answer, lad. Look at those stars eh? It's a great night to set sail, a great night for it. We'll follow those stars across the sea, all the way to France.'

I ran alongside him, trying to keep up as the horses started to pull away and the cart rolled slow and steady down the bumpy path. We jumped up onto the back and sat down facing the tunnel and the workhouse which become smaller and less clear as the horses picked up pace.

I looked up to watch the stars and saw my future set out before me. It was all in the stars now, all in the stars.

CHAPTER 37
NOAH

Beth has broken her leg in two places and she has mild concussion from the bang to her head. The paramedic tells Mr Bourne it is a clean break as they lift her stretcher up into the back of the ambulance. The doors shut but not before I see a small fragment of bone sticking out from her skin. Her blue jeans are ripped open and the paramedics are cutting them away from her legs as they shut the doors. And then I can't see her anymore just as the rain starts. The lights flash and the sirens sound as they pull out of the workhouse car park and head towards Halstead Hospital.

All I can see is blue and bone and blood.

And water.

I asked to go with her in the back of the ambulance but Mr Bourne said *no*, sending Miss Empingham instead. I have to travel back on the bus, at the front, on my own. I sit on a towel in my wet jeans with another towel wrapped around my arms and chest, which are covered in Beth's blood. My ripped and ruined baseball boots hang uselessly from my cold and battered feet. No one calls my name out on the silent return journey. No one whispers 'freak' down the bus. Sam sits behind me but doesn't speak to me, doesn't even ask if I'm alright, which is fine with me. I don't want to talk to anyone, not even Sam.

I close my eyes and keep them shut, seeing pictures of bones, ledges, steps and fast flowing water like a child's flashcards over and over, trying to show me something, to tell me something. I shiver and remember those two small squares of paper and the stubby blue biro from my mum's handbag. Did I prevent something or make things even worse? Again.

We are both visited at home by Mr Bourne. He comes straight round to my house after he's been to Beth's. My mum sits him down in the lounge and fusses over him, bringing cups of tea and homemade shortbread as if it was parents' evening again and we're on show. He tells us what happened at the workhouse.

'The heavy rainfall we've had has caused flash flooding, not just in our area, as I'm sure you've seen on the news. The trust at the workhouse have run their own investigation into the incident. They phoned me this morning to let me know what they think happened and will be sending us a report in due course.' He pauses to take a sip of tea.

'And of course the school will be looking into things as there were reports of the water pump being tampered with

231

or damaged, so leave that with me. The trust are going to brick up the old entrance or put a new door in but certainly replace the pipework, which was part of their long-term plans anyway.' He goes on and on about rain levels, risk assessment and new school policies. Mum and Dad nod their heads in a very serious manner. He keeps looking at me, praising me, saying words like *hero* and *admirable behaviour*. Mum and Dad smile back at him, agreeing with him. I can't stand it; I have to leave the room. I pick up a cup and mumble something about washing-up. I can't hear the rest from the kitchen but I've understood enough to get what happened down there, in the corpse tunnels.

Once he'd gone Mum and Dad call me back into the lounge for a chat.

'We need to talk.' They sit close to one another on the sofa, propping each other up. There's nothing worse than hearing '*we need to talk*'. It means they want to talk and I've got to listen. I throw myself down into the chair next to them and prepare myself for a lecture, for disappointment, for something unpleasant. So it comes as a bit of a shock when they launch into their 'talk' without doom in their voices.

'I've spoken to Beth's mum and we've come up with a bit of a plan. We've booked you in for some sessions with YoungMinds over the summer holidays.' Mum starts. I open my mouth to ask questions but she holds her hand up and carries on. Clearly this is the bit where I just get to listen.

'YoungMinds run art therapy sessions, so it's not as bad as you think before you start shutting down. They're a charity which helps young people dealing with … difficult issues, mental health issues. In the art sessions you can paint, use clay, sculpt and if you want to you can draw. Yes, Noah, you are allowed to draw. You've just got to start to control this, to understand it better and I think, and Dad does too, that they'll help you, more than we can anyway.' Mum stops to see if Dad wants to add anything. Apparently he does.

'This is all beyond us, we don't know what we're doing, mate, we need some help here,' Dad adds in support but then runs out of steam so Mum chips in again.

'Try to look at it as a place to talk about what you've done, what you've drawn or painted and I guess any problems you might be struggling with. As you know Rebecca, Beth's mum, is a GP and has sat in on a few sessions as part of a mental health course she went on. She was really impressed with what they do. So are we.'

They both stop talking. It all came out really fast, as if they thought I might just get up and leave before they'd got to the end of their speeches.

'I think it's the way forward. I know we've been burying our heads in the sand over this and that's not been very fair to you and I'm to blame for that. I'm sorry, mate, I really am,' Dad offers, his voice cracking on the last few words, and I can't open my mouth because I don't know what sound will come out. I force myself to look at the carpet; I can't look at them while they're saying stuff like this, being so nice and quiet. No shouting.

No being grounded.

No silent treatment.

No blame.

'And you are not to blame, for anything that's happened.' Dad adds, smiling at me.

I want to smile back but don't trust my face. I blink hard a few times and have a word with myself as I get to my feet, hoping this talk has come to an end but Mum has more to say. I sit back down.

'No, that's right, you're not to blame. None of us know why these things happen to you, love, none of it makes much sense but clearly there's something about you, something inside you that can … see things.' Mum isn't quite so well rehearsed now she is getting to the difficult bit that we've never managed to talk about before. We've always turned our backs on it, like a shadow.

'I think we thought that it was a one off, that the first time this happened was a fluke. To be honest, Noah, I couldn't really deal with it, not on top of Grace, too.' Dad's voice cuts out like a power cable pulled out. Mum takes over, clutching his hand in hers. They look nervous. My stomach rolls as I wait for the tide to turn, for their voices to go cold and hard now that her name is out there, hovering in the middle of the room like something about to detonate.

'We weren't able to think about what happened to you; we were both trying to deal with grief and loss and looking back, not dealing with it very well. I couldn't put the two things together because that would have made it all the worse, but this isn't going away and you're all we've got left, Noah. We loved Grace very much, so much … we love both of you so much and all we want … I just want you to be happy, love, happy and safe. We're going to keep you safe and help you to come to terms with this … with your *gift*.' I expected her to say curse not gift.

She offers the word to me like a present and holds her hand out to me. I take it.

Dad says, 'It's all about finding out, learning and working out a plan now, OK, mate? We're going to find out how to help you. We're in this together. We might not get it right, in fact, so far we've got a lot of it wrong, but we'll try again. We'll keep trying till we get it right.' He is in problem-solver mode. I wonder if he'll try and take my other hand and am a bit relieved when he doesn't. But I notice he doesn't say 'gift'. He wants to fix things, but at least he has realised there is something left to fix. At least he doesn't think I am completely broken.

'We're not saying things are going to all work out straight away and that this will be easy, because it won't.

But between the three of us we'll find a way, love. And don't forget, you saved her, Noah. You saved Beth and I'm really very proud of you.' Mum is standing in front of me now, pulling me up by my hands, not even wiping her tears away. I get up awkwardly and let her hug me. I rest my chin on her head and wrap my arms around her as she sniffs into my chest. And then Dad comes and stands behind me and holds us all. I can't see or breathe with my head buried somewhere underneath one of his arms, but I don't care. I listen to his heart beating steady and solid. I feel safe, for now anyway.

CHAPTER 38

THE HEDINGHAM HERALD
The Witchcraft case of Sible Hedingham
reaches its dramatic conclusion

Thomas Garland, a Farrier from Sible Hedingham, was summoned last week to speak against Emilia Rawlinson and Henry Hall for assaulting Blaze Ambroise, a boy between 14 or 15, also of Sible Hedingham. Complainant said, 'I heard a crowd of men led by Henry Hall coming up from the river. They were chasing a boy across the bridge and up into the high street making much noise and bother and threats. I did hear them chant "witch" over and over. The boy ran past my cottage and so I took him in. I took him in to my cottage and gave him food and drink. He was in fear of his life and couldn't speak, he was bruised and beaten. His clothes were wet and he had ropes around his wrists, as if he had been bound. I told the authorities what I'd seen and where he was. They came to my cottage and took him over to the Guardians. I had hoped they'd put him in the hospital first but they took him off to the infirmary at the Workhouse.'

Sentencing – Emilia Rawlinson and Henry Hall were charged with a criminal assault on Blaze Ambroise. Both Rawlinson and Hall were charged by the Superintendent before the magistrates at Castle Hedingham with having 'unlawfully assaulted a young boy known commonly as Blaze, with the intent of causing his death.' Some sensation has been excited by the near death of this little known foreigner, his case attracted much interest and the small courtroom at Castle Hedingham was packed.

A woman known as Jennifer White came forward during this time and said, 'I gave him the ring. The emerald was from me, it was my engagement ring. It never belonged to Emilia Rawlinson. She took it from him, she's the thief.' This stunning admission silenced the courtroom as Rawlinson was questioned and forced to admit her own deceit and theft with Hall as her accomplice.

Rawlinson and Hall were officially charged yesterday with attempt on the boy's life and the death of his dog whose body was found to be poisoned with arsenic. They were both tried at Chelmsford Assizes where they were found guilty, receiving six months hard labour. Neither Hall nor Rawlinson will be allowed to return to The Swan Inn, nor work or reside in the village of Sible Hedingham again.

ADDITION – Blaze Ambroise believed to be aged 14 or 15 was taken to Halstead Workhouse but disappeared from the same some days later. Records show that his mother, a Céline Ambroise died at Halstead Workhouse some two years ago.

The boy known as Blaze was in the habit of offering remedies and other potions to the sick in the village. The foreigner, possibly French, had no fixed abode but was said to live in a gardener's hut in the grounds of the still vacant Hedingham Manor. No reports of sightings of a Blaze Ambroise have been received at this time. No information is forthcoming about his whereabouts since he was reported missing from Halstead Workhouse.

More details regarding the probate case of the Manor House to follow.

Announcement – Death
Alfred Stoke (Alfie), shipman late of Sible Hedingham parish. Died setting out to sea during the Great Earthquake at Colchester, two other men were killed along with Stoke, the only survivor being Daniel White. The Stoke family and Alfred's fiancée Jennifer White and brother Daniel White ask for flowers to be left in the vestry at St Peter's.

Daniel White (Dan) has since returned to sea, setting sail for France and no longer resides in Sible Hedingham.

Announcement – Marriage
Married at St Peter's church, Mary Wright, daughter of

CHAPTER 39
NOAH

Beth's mum has set up a bed in the lounge, in front of the TV and the DVD player. *Edward Scissorhands* is playing. I pick up her copy of *Great Expectations* off the chair next to the sofa bed and sit down. Her mum says something about cups of tea and leaves us alone.

'You finally finished it then?' I ask, holding the worn and weary copy up to her.

'Yes. Pip forgives Estella. They walk off hand in hand into the sunset. *Happily ever after?*' she asks, another question hidden in the layers of this one.

'Yes, hand in hand. "He sees no shadow of another parting from her in their future." No more parting.' I offer my answer to her silent question, hoping it's the right one.

'It might be a while before I can walk off into any sunset but I can definitely hold your hand.' She smiles at me, poking her leg out of the bed. It is wrapped in a cast with some netting peeking out near her toes. I reach out my hand to cover them, they look cold. They've been painted a bright purple which suits her better than the dead blue colour. I don't know what to say, so keep looking around the room, half-heartedly watching the film, rubbing her toes.

'I never got the chance to say thank you,' she whispers, her eyes still on the screen watching Edward rest his chin on Kim's head as they hold one another, Edward taking great care not to hurt Kim.

'You don't have to thank me. I fell on you like a total idiot making things ten times worse. *I* probably broke your leg,' I reply, wishing things could just go back to normal.

'You saved me.' She begins taking my hand in hers. 'I thought I was going to *drown*, Noah.' She's determined to have her way and paint me as a hero.

The word cuts into me, I pull my hand out of hers.

'But I was there, you didn't … *drown*.' I choke on the word. I need to stop her. The music from the film is still building, violins and something twinkling like a child's merry-go-round. I want to turn it off, to silence it.

'Did they tell you what happened, Beth? It was just the water pipes; they got blocked by something and Mr Bourne said the pressure built up and it burst through the door and into the tunnel. Theo and Harley were messing around with the water pump, they probably broke it and left it running. Mr Bourne said something about flash floods all over the place too so…' I speak loud and clear, wanting her to think it was just one of those things like a random event or a natural disaster.

'Yep, he came to see Mum and Dad, who, by the way, think you are the best thing ever. They've been going on and on about you, said you saved my life. Mum said you are a hero. *I know! I know!*' She wrinkles her face up.

'Well, that's a first, a girl's parents actually liking her boyfriend.' I test out the word, feeling awkward. This time I pick up her hand.

'Yep. Must be a first. An all-time record. First time for everything … like you said.' She pulls me towards her, down to her lips. All thoughts about bones and bodies and corpse tunnels leave my mind for the first time in days as we kiss.

'They want to give you something, Mum and Dad, or show you their thanks. I think they're going to invite you and your parents round for Sunday lunch or something like that. My mum's been on the phone to your mum.'

Beth moves away from me to read my face. I feel the heat in my skin, burning. I don't care about Sunday lunch, I want to carry on kissing.

'Oh, they don't need to do that, tell them not to worry.' I lean back in to kiss her again.

'*Not to bother?* What? Well, *I* want you to come. I want to show you what you mean to me, what you did for me. I could have died, Noah. I keep having nightmares about it, about being trapped under the water, about gasping for air, they're horrible. I keep seeing bones and bodies floating by me in the water, hands reaching out to me with long fingernails trying to pull me down the steps under with them, trying to drown me.'

243

I can see where she's heading, but I have to stop her. I am not her hero. Heroes don't get stuff wrong. Heroes don't take too long to work stuff out. Heroes don't make stupid, *stupid* mistakes.

'Beth, just stop! Just stop for a minute … please?' I hear the wobble in my voice as I stand up and move away from her.

She pushes herself up in bed and stares across the room at me, annoyed.

'You wouldn't have *drowned*, please stop staying that, just stop saying that … word!' I can't keep the volume out of my voice. I am walking around the room, back and forth, not sure how I am going to explain. How am I going to show her how little she really knows about her *hero*?

'We used to live in a town called Buckingham. I was born there. It was nice and we had a lovely house with a long garden, a bit like yours actually but thinner. I used to spend all my time out there, in the sandpit and the paddling pool. We had a long cobbled path that wound around the garden and ended in a circle where all our stuff was, you know a slide, sandpit, a swing for two like a seesaw thing and the pool. I'd been running and tripped over on the cobbles. Mum told me off all the time about running on the path but I never listened. Dad kept saying he was going to replace it with a patio or gravel but he never did. I remember flying up into the air like I had wings, like I was a bird and it was really exciting, thrilling, for a second. Then I fell down and sent her crashing into the water. I landed next to Grace but on the rockery, not in the pool.'

Beth holds her hand up, as if we're in class, to ask me a question. I knew it was coming.

'Who's Grace?'

No. I can't say it yet. I have to keep going or I'll never get it all out.

'It was silent and so fast, too quick for me to scream or raise the alarm. I think I was winded cos I couldn't call for Mum or Dad. The pool was shallow but she must have banged her head because she didn't lift it out of the water. I remember I thought about pulling her long hair to raise her up out of the paddling pool. *She looked like a mermaid.* Noises kept coming in and out of my ears and my hands were asleep, sharp with pins and needles. I lay on my side like I was in an upside-down world with everything spinning. Speckles of light were in my eyes, I rubbed at them with my sun-creamed hand and I remember how much it *stung*. That's what I was thinking about! I was thinking about how much my bloody eyes stung!' I am so angry with myself, after all this time. I could live for a thousand years and never ever forgive myself.

'I kept my eyes closed.' I shut my eyes as I speak, remembering how my mother had run towards me, howling my sister's name '*Grace*' like a wild animal being torn apart. It was the worst sound she'd ever made.

'I said nothing. I was standing, rubbing my hands right into my eye sockets. I thought I could block it all out, that I could hide from what I'd drawn the day before. I could run away from the pictures I'd made. I could just *run away*. I remember standing there, crossing my fingers and wishing that the drawings in my toy box would just *fly away*!' I laugh and it's a nasty sound in the quiet room. I open my eyes but I don't dare look at Beth. I have to finish, there's one last bit to tell her. I have to tell her what I am.

I broke my family.

And I lost my sister.

'I didn't ever see her again. I'll *never* see her again. They took my sister away in an ambulance with my parents. They left a neighbour to watch me. Even though it was too late, they still took Grace to the hospital with the sirens on and the lights flashing blue. And then the storm broke, rain falling in my face almost sideways so I couldn't see the lights anymore and then they were gone.' I pause, remembering the crack of thunder, smelling the sharp rain, that tangy smell that's like nothing else, the lightning in the sky, an almost alien line of light across the navy blue skyline, leaving its mark.

'She'll always be three now, Grace. She's stuck at three and I can't even remember what she looked like. I have to sneak into Mum's room and look at photos of her. I can't hear her voice or her giggle, I can't remember what songs she liked me to sing, or what her favourite TV programme was, or if she preferred strawberry or vanilla ice cream, it's just all gone, washed away for ever.'

I sit back down on the sofa opposite her. I can't be near her. I can't be near anyone.

I thought I'd feel better. I thought I'd feel lighter, more honest. But I just feel empty, like all the words have gushed out of my mouth, which is now hanging open.

'Come here. Noah … I can't come to you, so you'll have to come to me. Come here, *please*?' Her voice is crackly and when I look up there are tears tracks on her cheeks. She holds her arms out to me.

I go to her. I fold myself carefully into her arms, taking care not to squash her or break any other part of her. She winds her arms around my back and pats me like I am a child who has fallen over. She speaks quietly to me, whispering in my ear.

'You couldn't save her, Noah. You couldn't have stopped it or understood it even, you were too little. Drawings couldn't have made any sense to you then. It wasn't your fault. You couldn't have saved … Grace. But you did save me. You got it this time.' She sounds triumphant at the end, as if she's just worked it all out for herself.

'But I broke your leg. I *hurt* you. I hurt *you* as well!' I stutter.

'No you didn't. The doctor said I broke it when I slipped on the steps, before you fell. You're not an actual giant, you know, you couldn't have broken my bones! You'd never hurt me, I know that even if you don't trust it yourself. *I know you.*' She wipes my eyes with her fingertips. I didn't even realise I was crying.

'Listen to me. You knew what would happen to me, didn't you? You drew it, you made sense of it, even if you didn't quite get it at the time. You knew as it happened. And then you stopped it happening. Yes, you did, *you* did. And you can do it again. That's what this means. You can do it again.'

I listen to her repeat herself, saying the same thing over and over as she rubs my back.

I saved her and who knows maybe I saved Eva's brother too? Maybe I am finally starting to make sense of this, or parts of it, anyway. Like a tessellation, there's a pattern to my drawings emerging. I've been able to see it all the time, but I'm only just starting to understand it. Maybe, if I look hard enough next time – *really hard* – a picture will develop.

EPILOGUE

Noah whistles softly to his dog who pads along the river path next to him. He hears the return call of a nightingale with its high, fast notes. The bird spreads out its wings and lifts upwards leaving the ground like heat rising.

Noah and his dog watch the bird hover over the river looking down at the slow moving water and then he sees it. The hand is right at the centre, fingers pushed together, palm upright. It is just where he knew it would be, waiting in the same place, warning him to stop. The river moves ever on around it as his breath catches in his throat.

And he stops. He listens this time. And he stops.

He stops breathing and waits for something to begin or for something to come to an end. The nightingale descends rapidly and the hand reaches out towards the bird as if to catch it, but just at the last moment the nightingale flicks its brown tail, flying away. Noah watches it soar into the clear blue sky, setting free the trapped air in his chest.

He turns back to the river just in time to see the fingers spread wide open before finally disappearing into the dark water. His big black dog barks a warning, an impatient sound and tugs insistently, pulling Noah towards the occupied bench and Beth sitting on it.

Noah walks quickly along the path towards her but he doesn't turn around. He doesn't look back, not once, because everything he needs to see is in front of him. His future is right there smiling at him and he knows this because he has drawn it.

AUTHOR'S NOTE

When I was writing the first draft of *Boy* I kept my eye
out for a strange village name to set the story in. I came
across Sible Hedingham and for some reason it jumped
out at me so in it went. Once I'd finished the first draft I
did a bit of research to make sure that Sible Hedingham
village fitted my story and that's when I found out about
Dummy and the real history of the village.

The last recorded case of swimming witches in England
occurred in the village of Sible Hedingham, Essex in 1863
when an elderly Frenchman, known locally by the name
of Dummy was dragged from the taproom in The Swan
public house to a nearby brook. The man gained a living
by telling fortunes and was a figure of curiosity in the
village. He was accused of bewitching Emma Smith. After
Dummy refused to 'remove the curse', Smith struck him
'several times' with a stick and pushed him into the brook
to 'swim him', encouraged by other villagers, in particular
master carpenter Samuel Stammers. Dummy died a few
days later in Halstead Workhouse from shock and
pneumonia caused by the constant immersion and ill-
treatment. Both Smith and Stammers were sentenced to
six months' hard labour. Although no longer a working

pub, The Swan Inn still stands and the stream in which Dummy was swum flows nearby.

I was shocked and spooked by the fact that a person much like Blaze existed and lived in the very village which I'd randomly picked for my setting, but it felt right and I'm a great believer in fate and destiny.

I spent a lot of time in two National Trust properties during the second and third drafts of *Boy* and found the atmosphere in both places incredibly helpful and stimulating when writing the scenes in the workhouse and in the tunnels. The workhouse at Southwell, Nottinghamshire is a strange place and I hope I've respectfully captured some of that strangeness in Blaze's chapters. I've visited a lot of National Trust properties through my role as an NT Writer in Residence, but I've never felt such a heavy presence and sensation in any of them as I did when I walked into the workhouse. I have to admit to feeling quite ill as I walked down the stone steps into the kitchens and thought about all those souls forced to walk through those gates and give up all their rights. The dormitories in particular were filled with a heavy atmosphere and strong sense of sadness lingering in the air. The building itself is a formidable testament to Victorian Britain and an extraordinary place to visit, one that I know I'll return to again.

The workhouse at Southwell doesn't have any tunnels (or at least not ones open to the public) so I've taken some liberties with Calke Abbey and their brewery tunnels and for the purposes of my novel placed them under *my* Halstead Workhouse. There was a workhouse at Halstead (there were over 700 workhouses in England during the Victorian era) but it no longer exists. Luckily for me, Southwell Workhouse does and has been impressively preserved.

I knew that many workhouses had tunnels underneath them and did a lot of research about workhouses in general, which led me to the horrific corpse tunnels and what happened to paupers in the workhouse once they died. The Anatomy Act of 1832 stipulated that paupers could be charged with the crime of poverty. Before this the Murder Act of 1752 stated that only the corpses of executed murderers could be used for dissection. After 1832, bodies could be dissected as a way to repay welfare debt unless family members could pay to reclaim the body. As you can imagine, most workhouse inmates didn't have the means to buy bodies back.

The brewery tunnels at Calke Abbey are very long, dark and quite creepy. They fitted the purposes of my book beautifully and became my corpse tunnels. What happened to Noah and Beth down there was inspired by something that happened to me on my first and last visit to Calke Abbey tunnels, but that's another story.
http://www.nationaltrust.org.uk/workhouse-southwell/
http://www.nationaltrust.org.uk/calke-abbey/

The real Colchester Earthquake happened in 1884 not 1865, as I have suggested in the newspaper article in this novel.

YoungMinds – YoungMinds is the UK's leading charity committed to improving the emotional wellbeing and mental health of children and young people. Details about their art therapy courses can be found on their website – http://www.youngminds.org.uk/about